DEATH OF A SAPLING

Jay Larkin

To C.
My Rock

With thanks to:
Jackie Bates for editorial input
Anna Churnin and Barbara Sopkin for help and support

CONTENTS

CHAPTER 1

As she turned off the main road and drove through the black-painted iron gates, Kate shivered. Her heart beat faster as she read the sign. 'Sapplewood Independent School' was painted in subdued gold letters on a navy-blue background. 'Boarding for Boys Aged 13 to 18.' Bodoni typeface, she registered automatically.

The long drive bordered by grassy banks was the epitome of one found in a well-kept English country house, looking its best in the sunshine. Yet she found her foot releasing the accelerator to slow down the car. It took a conscious effort to continue. Gripping the steering wheel, her heart racing, she forced herself to drive on.

What was the matter? The entrance seemed familiar, but she'd never been there before, and wasn't prone to episodes of deja vu. Such an imposing place had probably been used as a TV location, which must be why she recognised it. The sweeping drive led to an equally impressive building in the Palladian style.

Kate pulled up outside the entrance, where a row of pillars supported a triangular pediment. The graceful, white building was reminiscent of a Greek temple. Her hands grew clammy and a trickle of sweat ran down her spine as she looked at it. An unaccountable feeling of dread tightened her chest. She saw a handwritten sign attached to the pillar at the end, 'Pottery Course' with an arrow. Switching the engine back on, she followed the signs round the side of the building, her heart still thumping.

Starting a residential course in an unfamiliar place, with unknown participants, Kate already felt a certain degree of concern. As she drove on, she exhaled and her hands relaxed their grip on the steering wheel. When she arrived at the pottery studio, the feelings of anxiety slowly subsided. She sat in the car for a few minutes before she could take in her surroundings. In contrast to the substantial, classical architecture of the main building, the pottery studio was a one storey, modern structure of glass and wood. She got out of the car and grabbed her rucksack.

There were several other cars parked nearby, and a man was leaning into the boot of an elderly Volvo. He straightened up, carrying a bag. He was solidly built, with a fringe of grey hair surrounding his bald head like a tonsure, and rosy cheeks. He smiled at her.

"A fellow student, I hope?" he said with a pronounced northern accent.

She managed a smile and nodded.

"Kate Fielding."

"Henry Applegate."

They walked towards the studio and when they reached the entrance, Henry held the door open with a flourish.

"Age before beauty," she said as she stepped through, and his face creased into a grin. He was clearly old enough to be her father and appreciated the joke. It was reassuring to enter the pottery studio with an ally. She wondered what to expect.

There were five others in the room, two women, two teenage boys and a slim bearded man with black hair pulled back in a ponytail. He spoke.

"Welcome everyone, glad you could make it, I'm Adam Trayne.

The Artist in Residence at Sapplewood School. Really, Potter in Residence. You may've come across my work in galleries around the country. I work with the pupils – the boys – and the school lets me run these courses in the holidays."

Kate nodded; Adam had been recommended as a well-known potter with a no-nonsense approach to teaching.

"Help yourself to drinks and we'll get going." He pointed at an area in the corner with a kettle and an assortment of handmade mugs.

Kate, Henry and the four others sat down on chairs laid out in a semi-circle. Adam faced them.

"Let's introduce ourselves – first names only. We're all equal, we're all potters. Some of us are further along the road than others, but we're on the same journey.

You'll each have your own wheel and as much clay as you need. In my experience, there's no magic way to improve – just practice. You can spend all day throwing. I'll be going round, so just ask for help if you need it. I'll also be giving demonstrations. You can watch if you want – I won't be offended if you don't. The group's small to make sure I can give everyone enough attention. I'll show you where things are, we'll have lunch and then get started."

The two other women introduced themselves as Dani – about ten years older than Kate, short with shoulder length blonde hair and Fearne, who had well cut grey hair and red framed glasses. The boys were sixth formers who lived abroad, and stayed at the school for the half term week.

At the back, the pottery studio led out to a courtyard with wooden tables and benches. Here a picnic lunch was laid out. The schoolboys sat at a table away from the others and spoke mainly to each other.

Kate found out more about Henry. An art teacher at a secondary school, he'd taken early retirement at the beginning of the year.

He was staying at the same nearby farm as she was.

Adam talked to each student individually.

"What're you hoping to get out of the course?" he asked Kate.

"I've been doing a pottery evening class, but there aren't enough wheels for all of us. I just can't get the hang of throwing, but I really want to."

 He nodded at her reply.

"Take your time, be patient. I haven't had a student who didn't learn to throw by the end of the week. Watch the first demo, and I'll go through the steps with you."

Kate viewed Adam's demonstration of the basic technique of throwing, turning a lump of clay into a symmetrical vessel. He made it look so easy, but under her hands, the clay had always refused to behave. The other students seemed to be more advanced than her, confidently placing lumps of clay on their wheels and getting started. She hesitated and Adam came over to her.

"I've already forgotten everything you showed us," she said.

"No problem, I'll run through it again."

Adam's calm, reassuring approach gave her confidence. She had to concentrate completely or lose control of the clay. It was like learning to drive a car, Adam assured her, later the actions would become automatic.

The afternoon flew by and at five Kate washed her hands and untied her clay-spattered apron.

"Good work, well done everyone," said Adam, "if anyone wants to join me, I'll be in the pub in the village at eight."

Kate drove away from the pottery studio, following the lane towards the main school. As she passed this striking building and approached the entrance gates, another wave of fear washed over her, and she found herself clenching her jaw. Once again she required an effort of will to continue. Turning into the main road, she breathed out, realising she'd been holding her breath. The tension in her body receded, but an unsettling tag of memory still tugged at her mind. She hadn't experienced this scene on screen – she'd been there before. But when? Why? She pondered these questions as she drove to the farm.

Henry was waiting outside.

"Where were you planning to eat?"

"I don't know. Maybe grab something at the pub. What about you?"

"That sounds like a good idea, let's meet at seven. I'll drive, no sense in taking two cars."

Kate's room wasn't large, but there was a view over the fields, which would have been charming on a brighter day. However, now a mass of dark clouds heralded rain. After a shower, she relaxed on the bed, catching up on emails and social media.

When Kate came downstairs she found Henry waiting in the hall, wearing a brightly coloured sou'wester. She hid a smile. He looked like a shiny yellow ball.

"It's pouring out there," he said, "Are you sure you want to go? That jacket doesn't look waterproof – you'll get soaked by the time we reach the car."

"It's supposed to be showerproof. Anyway, I'm starving."

Henry was correct in his prediction, and wet through, Kate shivered as they entered the pub. It was a typical country hostelry, complete with generous fire in the inglenook fireplace. They sat at a table near the fire and Kate stretched out her hands to the blaze.

"No salad for me tonight," Henry said studying the menu, "steak and kidney pie and mash."

"I wouldn't have said you were a salad man," Kate said.

"What are you implying?" he said, pretending to be offended, "it's no easy job maintaining this svelte figure, I can tell you."

They both laughed. Kate ordered the same, and over the meal, she learned about Henry's wife and grown-up son. He clearly loved his work and had returned to the school to run a crafts club after he officially retired.

"That's why I want to brush up on my pottery. Wonderful facilities at Sapplewood, but then it's a private school. I've always worked in ordinary state schools."

Henry was equally interested in hearing about Kate. She told him about her evening class and an unsuccessful painting course she'd been on the year before in Devon.

"I'm sure this is going to be much better; Adam's well organised – that was the problem last time. We wasted a lot of time while the teacher got things set up."

He nodded.

"Most important for a teacher, being organised."

"I wonder if the others will brave the weather?" he said when they'd finished their meal.

They scanned the entrance as they sipped coffee, watching a few dripping bedraggled drinkers arrive. However, the potters were made of sterner stuff and a figure in a long black coat came in, called out a greeting and approached their table. They couldn't make out who it was at first, as the hood obscured the wearer's face. A hand pulled it back to reveal Adam.

"Now that's what I call a coat," said Henry, "much cooler than my sou'wester. Just what you need for this weather."

"It's Australian – made of oilskin," Adam said.

"With the wide sleeves and that sort of cape thing, you look like Batman," Kate said.

Adam smiled.

"I prefer Spiderman myself," he said, shaking the rain off his coat.

"In my sou'wester I look more like SuperTed than Superman," said Henry screwing up his face.

Fearne was the next to arrive.

"I'm staying with friends who live nearby, so I'll spend my evenings with them, but I wanted to meet up tonight with everybody," she said.

Soon Dani turned up and everyone relaxed over drinks. Henry had a disarming sense of humour and was genuinely interested in people. He asked everyone about their jobs and where they lived.

"I live in a village outside Cambridge and I work in a lab. I can't say any more, it's top secret," Dani said.

Henry's eyes opened wide.

"Research for the government, Official Secrets Act and all that?"

Dani laughed.

"No, a pharmaceutical company, industrial espionage actually."

"Why are you doing the course?" Fearne said.

"I've been collecting teapots for years and I wanted to learn how to make them. I've been doing an evening class and my husband bought me a wheel. I thought this course would give me a boost to get started on my own."

"Your turn, Kate, tell us what you do," said Dani.

"I'm a freelance graphic designer. I work from home in London and I try and go on art or craft breaks every year to recharge my batteries. I've also been doing a pottery evening class, but I'm not making any progress."

Adam looked at her thoughtfully.

"I'm a journalist for a local paper," said Fearne, "I live in Deal, on the Kent coast. I did a one day throwing course and loved it. This seemed like the next step."

After a lull in the conversation, Dani changed the subject, frowning as she spoke.

"I'm sure I've heard about Sapplewood School before – but I can't remember why."

Adam picked up his glass and took a swig of beer without speaking.

"Yes," she went on "wasn't there an accident there – a year or so ago – someone died?"

Adam swallowed his mouthful and spoke reluctantly.

"Yes. A boy – one of the pupils – had a fall."

Dani ignored his discomfort.

"What exactly happened?"

"We don't like to talk about it around here," said Adam quietly, "He got hold of alcohol. He got drunk and did something stupid and dangerous. There was an accident. He died."

Everyone tutted and looked shocked. Adam checked his watch, excused himself and left. Once he'd gone, the others discussed the incident. The girl clearing away glasses, heard what they were saying and joined in.

"It was awful. He was a good-looking boy. They said he got drunk and fell out of the bell tower. In the chapel."

"Was he alone?" asked the incorrigible Dani.

"That's what they said."

A well-built man who was obviously the landlord came over.

"Good evening all, welcome to the White Hart. You must be Adam's new students. Thirsty work making pots," he said with a smile, then turned to the girl.

"Tara, don't stand here chatting, there's tables need clearing."

She moved away.

"I hear you've been talking about the boy who died – shocking business." He shook his head, "But that place – the school – there's something about it. That's not the first accident there's been. I've told my girls to keep away from those woods at night. I'd advise you folks the same."

His words silenced the group.

"That seems to be the end of that," Henry said after a pause, "ready to go, Kate?"

As they were getting into the car, Dani came running out of the pub.

"Kate," she said breathlessly, "is this your bag, it was under your seat?"

"Yes, thanks so much. I'm always forgetting things."

"Lucky she spotted it," Henry said raising his eyebrows.

Just as they arrived back at the farm, a small car pulled up behind them and Dani got out – she was also staying there. There was laughter all round and cheerful goodnights.

Although tired, Kate didn't fall asleep easily. She tossed and turned in the unfamiliar bed and unaccustomed quiet of her surroundings. Recalling the drive to Sapplewood and the entrance to the school, she experienced once again the feelings of unease and dread, albeit in a milder form. What could be the reason? The school buildings and its grounds seemed perfectly pleasant. Innocuous. Something had disturbed her. If she hadn't been there before...

She opened her eyes and sat up with a start. The story of the boy falling to his death at the school. Could that have affected her? But the feeling had come first. She only heard of the accident afterwards. In the night, strange fancies, shrugged off in daylight, carry more weight. Might the tragic accident have somehow caused bad vibes, and a negative atmosphere around the school? What nonsense – she'd never given a moment's credence to such an idea before. When she finally drifted off to sleep, however, her dreams were haunted by a faceless boy endlessly tumbling out of a high tower in the dark.

The following morning all the potters were eager to get going. Kate tried to remember what Adam had said and put it into practise. However, one after another, three of her attempts were thrown into the clay bin. Adam came over and Kate showed him what she was doing, feeling as if all eyes were on her. He adjusted the position of her hands. For the first time she was able to keep the clay centred on the wheel – an essential action – and hollowed out the middle. She formed the walls, ending up with a reasonable pot and sat back in relief and satisfaction.

After coffee, Adam demonstrated how to form the handle of a vessel, by pulling or stretching a roll of clay. This was a completely different technique to throwing. Everyone had a go, although Kate couldn't imagine making a mug worthy of a handle. But to her surprise, she manipulated the clay with ease and the result was pronounced perfect by Adam, while the others struggled. This small achievement gave her confidence. At least there was something she could do well.

At lunchtime, to her surprise, Adam asked her to join him at a separate table, away from the group.

"You said last night you're a graphic designer?"

"Yes, I am."

"The headmaster, of the school, he needs one, a graphic designer. He hired someone to do a job, but they backed out. He's in a bit of a spot."

She waited for him to continue.

"I wondered if you were interested."

She frowned.

"What kind of job is it?"

"Rebranding they call it. Designing a new prospectus, website. I told him I'd ask you."

Taken by surprise, she thought about his request. Her policy was never to turn down work without looking into it properly.

"I might be. What exactly would it involve?"

"I don't know the details, but you could talk to Mr Radcliffe."

"It'd be better if I could see the brief first – I wouldn't want to waste his time."

"No problem, I'll speak to him."

In the afternoon, Kate successfully threw two more pots and finished on a high.

"What're we doing tonight?" Henry asked Kate and Dani at the end of the session, taking it for granted they would be together.

"Let's ask at the farm if there's another pub in the area we can try," Dani said and they agreed.

After a shower, Kate checked her emails. The brief for the graphic design job at the school had arrived, and she went through it. It seemed straightforward and similar to a previous project she'd done for a homoeopathy college. Did she have the time, with her other commitments? In the end, it came down to hard cash. She'd no idea if the school were au fait with current rates, however, they'd agreed a figure with another designer, so it was worth finding out more about it. She sent Adam a message, and he replied saying the headmaster would meet her in his study at lunchtime the following day.

She came downstairs to find Henry and Dani conferring with Barbara, their landlady, about another pub.

"You walk across the fields in that direction," she said, "here are a couple of torches."

Kate looked puzzled, why would they need torches? She soon found out. Away from the farmhouse, the moon hidden by clouds, the fields were pitch dark. She was shocked.

"You are such a townie," said Dani, laughing, "take a torch and point it towards the ground as you go, so you don't trip over anything."

It was unnerving walking in the darkness, with only small beams to guide them. Kate picked her way gingerly.

"What about rabbit holes?" she said, "I can't see them in the grass..."

"There are more rabbit holes on the Internet than in these fields," said Henry.

The others laughed, but the laughter was good humoured and Henry walked beside Kate. The pub was worth the walk, serving better food in more upmarket surroundings than the other. The group had an enjoyable evening and arrived back at the farm without any mishaps. It was still early, so the three of them settled down in the snug – a small room reserved for guests – where there was a kettle, fridge and a microwave.

"I asked Barbara about the boy who had the accident at the school," said Dani, "she told me he was sixteen and his name was Max. My son's that age – makes you think doesn't it?" Neither of the others commented, but she went on. "You'd think, sending a boy to a fancy school like that – all the facilities – acres of grounds, best teachers, you'd think that'd be a dream come true – give him the best start in life." She sighed. "You never know what goes on in these places. Some of the teachers might be perverts – with the boys sleeping there. My Ben's school might be an ordinary comprehensive, but at least he's safe."

Kate had nothing to say and Henry who probably could contribute, also stayed silent.

"I think I'll give Neil and the kids a call," Dani said and she stood up. "Night all."

"Another cuppa?" Henry asked and Kate nodded. "Let's talk about something else," he said handing her a cup, "you can call me nosy and slap my face, but I am nosy. What were you and Adam talking about so seriously?"

Kate couldn't be offended, Henry had the expression of an eager, elderly schoolboy.

"Well," she said slowly, "he made a proposition."

"Not an improper one, I hope?" he said, his eyes creasing and his mouth turning up at the edges.

She laughed and told him the story.

"Will you take the job?"

"If they'll give me enough time – and pay well of course."

"There's no shortage of money at that school. If they're willing to spend it."

Kate was afraid her newly acquired pot-throwing skills would vanish overnight, but next morning she produced two more successful pots, and started to enjoy the process.

At lunchtime, she changed out of her jeans and picked up her laptop.

"Where's the headmaster's office?" she asked Adam.

"In the main building, there's a sign in the lobby, you can't miss it."

There were few people around in the main building and Kate took in the historic atmosphere and fine architecture. No doubt the place would have quite a different feel when the pupils returned. She entered a room where a middle-aged woman was sitting at a desk, piled high with an untidy collection of papers. A pair of glasses was perched on her head and her hair was pulled back in a messy bun, with several strands hanging down on either side of her face. The woman nodded in the direction of an inner door.

"He's expecting you," she said, pushing the fugitive wisps of hair behind her ears.

Kate knocked on the door and it was opened by a tall man who cut an impressive figure in a flowing black gown over his dark suit.

"Coffee, please, Mrs Anderson," he said to the seated woman, who sighed loudly, pulled off her glasses and threw them onto her desk, where they disappeared among the debris.

"Come through, Miss er…"

"Fielding. Kate Fielding."

"Giles Radcliffe."

They shook hands. The room contained a massive dark wood desk and two chairs. The furniture was old fashioned but of solid quality. Mr Radcliffe pointed to an imposing portrait on the wall behind him.

"Our founder, Sir James Mottram," he said clasping his hands together as if in prayer.

A man in Victorian clothes, a bushy beard and a serious expression stared over Kate's head.

"Please take a seat."

The door opened and Mrs Anderson entered carrying a tray with two cups of coffee. She placed it on the table none too gently and the coffee slopped into the saucers.

"Miss Fielding, the purpose of this exercise is to update the image of our venerable establishment. Sapplewood School has been a centre of excellence in education since its foundation in the nineteenth century. We delight in those traditions that keep the spirit of the school alive without constraining us from embracing modern day life.

"To this end, over the last few years, we've carried out developments and improvements to the school. Now we need an up-to-date image – prospectus, website – and so forth to reflect our current brand." His unctuous, expansive manner gave the impression Kate was a prospective parent to whom he was selling the school. "Do you have experience of this type of project?"

On her laptop, Kate brought up examples of her work for the homoeopathy college. Mr Radcliffe studied the screen.

"Excellent, most attractive. Just the kind of thing we are looking for. Would this project be of interest to you?"

"Possibly," she said, "but I have some questions. Firstly, what time period are you thinking of – I do have other work currently?"

"Of course," said the headmaster, "we'd need to have it completed within two months."

"Do you have any material I can use?"

"Yes, we've had a set of new photographs taken of the pupils, the buildings and the grounds."

"That would help, but I need to get to know the school when the pupils are around, to get a feel of the atmosphere. I spent a few days at the homeopathy school – it was really useful."

The head sat back in his chair and his brow furrowed.

"If you're willing, you could stay at the school. We'd provide accommodation, a study bedroom, meals…"

"That'd certainly help, if I could have access to the buildings and talk to the pupils."

"Of course, of course," said the head.

"I haven't seen round the school properly yet," she said thoughtfully, "but I'm really impressed with the ceramics studio. A brand-new building, great equipment – there can't be many other schools with facilities like that."

Mr Radcliffe frowned.

"That's true, but the sort of parents we're after are not interested in pottery. Those parents would form the impression that it was our main focus, to the detriment of other subjects. They don't want their boys to come out of school as potters!

"We had a generous donation from an old boy. I would've preferred to spend it on other facilities, but the donor insisted the money was to be used to create a ceramics studio. Those were the conditions of the gift. The endowment also covered initial payment for an Artist in Residence." He shrugged. "We weren't going to look the proverbial gift horse in the mouth, but frankly the money would've been much better spent elsewhere. So, in short, don't make a big feature of the ceramics."

She thought about his words. How strange that an alumnus of the school would endow a ceramics studio, of all things.

"But all this supposes, Miss Fielding, that you're willing to take the job."

As they hadn't mentioned payment, she took the bull by the horns.

"And how much would you be paying?"

Mr Radcliffe mentioned a sum larger than Kate would've quoted. "Would that be acceptable?"

She sat back. The money was good, she could do the work in the timeframe, and yet... The project would be interesting and she could produce a high-quality result. But something held her back. She knew nothing about children, how did she really feel about staying at the school? No, that wasn't the problem. The same vague feeling of unease Kate had experienced when she first arrived at the school, lurked at the back of her mind. And Giles Radcliffe – she hadn't warmed to him. But if she only worked for clients she liked...

She sat up straight. It'd be foolish to turn down this job on a whim. She had to think ahead, be strategic. If she achieved a successful outcome, rebranding other educational institutions could be a useful niche market.

"Thank you very much for the offer, Mr Radcliffe, I'm happy to accept."

"Excellent, I'm delighted."

She returned to her laptop and brought up on screen her usual form of contract. "I'll e-mail this to you now, please could you print it off so we can both sign."

"Yes, yes."

He stood up, went out and spoke to Mrs Anderson. "So sorry, there's a problem with our printer at the moment. Mrs Anderson will do it as soon as possible. When will you be able to start?"

"The pottery course finishes on Thursday afternoon; I'll go home for the weekend and collect my stuff. When do the pupils come back to the school?"

"Sunday afternoon. Would you be able to return on Monday morning?"

"Yes, that'd be fine."

Walking back to the studio, Kate still wasn't sure she'd made the right decision. What would Luke say when he heard she'd be working in a boys' boarding school?

When she'd changed back into her jeans, Kate realised she'd left her laptop in Mr Radcliffe's office. Only a few months before, she'd lost her iPad on the train and had resolved to be more careful with her possessions. Annoyed at her carelessness, she went back to the headmaster's office. Mrs Anderson's back was turned and Mr Radcliffe's door was open, so she slipped into his room. The laptop was lying on the table. She picked it up and walked quietly out.

Back in the lobby she stopped suddenly. In Mrs Anderson's office, she'd heard a sound. It was the whirring of a printer. The printer that Mr Radcliffe said wasn't working.

After lunch, as Kate struggled to form a pot, the clay rebelled, refusing to accept her authority. Adam watched her throw the misshapen lump into the clay bin.

"I've lost the knack," she said, angry at herself.

"No, you haven't, you're not concentrating. That often happens. Let's change things. What would you really like to make now?"

"A mug," she replied without hesitation.

"No problem, let's try that." Adam threw a mug, explaining what he was doing, under Kate's watchful eyes. She had a go and the magic returned. A perfect cylinder rapidly emerged.

"Well done, now what?"

"Lots more mugs."

"If you make the mugs today, you can put on the handles tomorrow. How was the meeting with Radcliffe?"

"I've got the job. Thanks. You'll be seeing me next week – I'm coming back to stay for a while to find out about the school."

Adam frowned.

"Is that normal?"

"I don't know, but it'll be helpful for me."

He looked as if he was about to say something else, but pressed his lips together and turned away.

Kate spent the afternoon producing mug after mug. Adam demonstrated how to make the spout on a teapot, but she didn't stop. She looked up in surprise to see the others taking off their aprons. The afternoon had vanished, but she had the mugs to show for her work. She carefully turned them upside down on a shelf to dry.

"Where are we going tonight, gang?" Henry asked.

"My vote says no more walking through pitch black fields," said Kate with feeling and the other two laughed.

Henry had heard of a rustic pub about twenty minutes away in the car, and Dani offered to drive. When he saw the small, two-door car he sighed.

"I'm not sure I'll fit in," he said in mock dismay, "and if I do get in, I'm positive I'll never get out again!"

The laughter that followed set the tone for the first part of the evening. Henry insisted on giving directions, saying he didn't believe in satnavs, but after driving for at least half an hour, Kate said in a plaintive voice.

"I remember that tree. I think we've been past here before. You've done this on purpose."

"Yes, now you're both in my power. You can't get away."

"You mean you can't get away from us," said Dani. In the end, more by luck than judgement, they found the elusive hostelry. It was rustic – but self-consciously so. The menu described every dish in excruciatingly pretentious terms, which was a further source of merriment.

"I'll have the blonde haricots in a coulis of tomatoes, on a raft of grilled bruschetta – beans on toast to you," Henry chortled.

They were starving and the dishes took as long to prepare as their overcomplicated descriptions suggested, so quality went unnoticed as the three polished off their meals.

"Anyone for pudding?" asked Dani.

"Only if they've got hand sliced pieces of the finest brioche covered in Normandy butter, soaked in a vanilla cream and baked until crisp." said Henry. When the others look puzzled, he added,

"Bread and butter pudding."

When they arrived back at the farm, they made for the snug. The mood had altered and Dani returned to her favourite topic, the boy who fell to his death.

"Barbara told me he was alone when it happened. I can't understand why. I know from Ben – they do things – get up to mischief – with their mates. Drinking and fooling around – they egg each other on. The only way I can see it happening if he was alone, was if he meant to... you know... he wanted to... kill himself. And that's awful. Shows how desperate he was – unhappy. And the school didn't help him. If my son was upset like that, I'd know. A mum knows."

Henry said nothing and Kate tried to put an end to the subject.

"I can't say anything. I don't have kids, or even nieces or nephews. I've no idea how a teenage boy would behave or feel."

Henry spoke firmly.

"I've taught teenagers for thirty years, and what I say is, you don't know. The things they get up to never cease to amaze me. We don't know the facts in this case. It's not helpful to speculate."

Dani frowned as if offended by Henry's tone. She stood up.

"I'm going to call my Ben and go to bed."

"Now I've done it," said Henry, filling up the kettle, "I suppose she won't speak to me."

"You were quite right. Going over it like that feels ghoulish to me." Even more than that, speculating about the accident brought back Kate's feelings of unease and anxiety.

"Anyway, what happened about your job?" he said.

She told him about the meeting.

"So, you'll be coming back here next week?" he asked.

"It looks like it. At least for a few days. It's the only way to do the job properly."

"That's a turn up for the books," his eyes creased, "I'll be around as well."

"What do you mean?"

"I haven't told you the whole story – how I came to be in this neck of the woods at the moment."

"Wasn't it for the pottery course?"

"Yes, but there's more to it. As I told you, we've always lived up north – my wife, Sandra and me. I didn't tell you that she's younger than me and a lot cleverer." He said this in a matter-of-fact tone. "She's the vice principal of a college. Our son, Andrew, went to university down south and stayed there. He got married and last year they had their first child – our grandson – a lovely little lad.

"They wanted to see more of us, started saying we should move nearer them. I think it was free babysitting they wanted," he said with a grin, "anyway, we thought about it. I was already set to take early retirement. Sandra saw a job advertised, as principal of a college near here, a step up for her. She applied for it on a whim – and got it. Suddenly it was all happening.

"Now we have to find a house down here. It's not easy, because prices are so much higher. We came down for a weekend to have a look – that's when I heard about this course. This area is a bit cheaper than Andrew's, but not too far from them. There's not much time, Sandra's starting the new job in a few months. So, I'm going home this weekend, but I'm coming back on Monday – to stay until I find something."

"That's a surprise. Where're you staying?"

"Luckily, Barbara said my room's available for the next couple of weeks. It's the cheapest way to do it. I can't stay with Andrew, it's too much for them with the little one."

Kate took in the news.

"I'm so pleased, for myself, I mean. It'll be nice to have a friend nearby. I'm rather dreading staying at the school. But with you around..."

"Don't worry, another few days and you'll be sick of the sight of me."

They both smiled.

"I won't be going out for meals every night – can't afford it, Barbara said I can use this fridge and microwave."

"I won't either – the school's providing my meals."

He yawned. "Time for beddibyes. See you tomorrow, Kate."

The next morning Kate finished the mugs she'd made.

"Leave them here and I'll fire them in the kiln next week," Adam said, "we might be able to get them glazed as well while you're here."

All the participants were pleased with what they'd produced during the course, and slackened off during the morning, sitting around and chatting. The course officially finished at lunchtime and the two pupils from the school vanished. The others stayed for their last picnic lunch. As they ate, Adam was in an extremely good mood, smiling and laughing.

"I know you'll be glad to get rid of us," Henry said putting on an offended expression, "but you don't need to make it so obvious."

Adam looked puzzled.

"You've been grinning to yourself for the last hour," said Henry.

"It's not that. I've just had some news I've been waiting for. Now it's official I can tell you."

The group looked at him expectantly.

"A TV company are doing a new series about pottery. I'm going to be the resident expert. Eight episodes and more if it takes off."

There were congratulations all round.

"It's good for the craft," Adam said, "a TV show will put pottery on the map."

"When you're a household name and big star don't forget us," Henry said, "don't forget where you came from." He slapped Adam on the back.

"When do you start work?" Kate asked.

"At the end of the school year, July."

"Will you still carry on working here and running the courses?"

"I'm not sure. It won't be full time, but the money's good. It's time for a change."

Goodbyes were said and Kate, Henry, Fearne and Dani exchanged contact details.

Kate drove back past the main school building and out through the black painted iron gates. She'd done this so many times now, she no longer experienced the strong feeling of dread, just a momentary twinge of unease. Then she was on her way home.

CHAPTER 2

Whenever Luke was in the country, their ritual was Saturday lunch together. Kate had known Luke since their childhood. Although he was four years older, their parents had been friends for years, and they spent a lot of time together during the school holidays because his father worked for the Foreign Office and was often posted abroad. It'd been like having an older brother - except none of her friends had such good relationships with their older brothers.

Now... it was something more. Their relationship had never been defined and she wasn't sure how he felt about her. She never asked, fearing to spoil their friendship.

This time he was coming over to her place. In the morning she was busy doing chores, resulting both from her time away at the pottery course, and in preparation for her stay at school the following week, and she had no time to cook. Luke was a vegetarian, so she bought a quiche from the local artisan bakery and salads and cheese from the Greek deli.

Each time she saw Luke again, the first thing Kate noticed was his tan. He wasn't a sun worshipper, but his work – providing relief for people in crisis –invariably occurred in a scorching climate. His chestnut hair had not yet received its English trim, and curled around his neck. They hugged and she felt his bones, he was always at his thinnest when he returned from a trip.

She watched him eat.

"You're half starved."

"The food out there's not exactly... gourmet," he said, helping himself to more, "This quiche is awesome."

Kate frowned.

"Awesome? I thought you were in Tanzania not Texas."

Luke grinned.

"One of the team is from the US. I guess I picked up some super cool words," he said in an exaggerated accent.

They both laughed.

"Besides, you get so caught up in the work, there's so much to do, eating seems unimportant."

He never talked about his work in detail. Those in between periods in England helped him recharge, so he didn't want to think about it.

"What about you, Katie, what have you been up to? Anything interesting?"

She told him about the pottery course and showed him pictures on her phone of the mugs she'd made.

"I'm no expert," he said, "but they look professional to me."

She smiled.

"We had a good teacher. I got the hang of it, the knack. It's satisfying to make something useful – not just decorative. I'd love to get my own wheel if I had the space."

She brought over coffee.

"The pottery course actually led to a job. You'll never guess where I'll be working next week."

After a couple of wild guesses, she explained.

"At a boys' boarding school."

"What?" He looked at her, his spoon in the sugar bowl. "How come?"

"I'm designing publicity material for the school – prospectus, website that kind of thing. Sapplewood School."

Luke was emptying the sugar from his spoon into his cup as she spoke. The spoon dropped out of his hands and his cup fell over on the wooden table with a crash. He didn't move. Kate soaked up the pool of liquid with a paper napkin and ran for a cloth.

As she cleared up the mess, he looked at her. His lips were pale against the tan.

"What did you say?"

"I said I'll be working at Sapplewood School, and staying there for a few days."

He grabbed the arms of his chair and she watched his knuckles turn white. His whole body was rigid.

"Are you okay?"

He nodded.

"Just a minute, I…"

She poured him a glass of water and he drank.

"You don't remember?" He looked at her, his brow furrowed.

"Remember what?"

"About the school – that school?"

"No, should I?" She stared into his eyes. "You're scaring me. What's this about?"

He passed his tongue over dry lips.

"I don't want to talk about it. I can't. It's hard. Kate – you really don't remember?"

"No, I don't."

He took a deep breath and leaned towards her.

"Do you remember that I was at boarding school, here in England. When my folks were in Japan?"

"Yes of course. You came when you were about twelve, because there were no suitable schools out there.

He nodded.

"Yes, that's right. I had to go to boarding school here. The first school I went to was Chilton Abbey. It was hard at first, I was homesick, but I soon settled down. I made friends; the teachers were nice – mostly. I liked the sports, did well."

"Yes, we came to visit you." she screwed up her eyes. "Sports day, was it? We had a picnic in the grounds. And one time we took you out for lunch. Weren't you in a play?"

"Yes, that's right. I remember. And sometimes I stayed with you, for half term if it wasn't worth travelling back to Japan. I was there for about three years, but something happened and the school closed down suddenly. I had nowhere to go. My parents weren't on the spot. Your parents tried to help, but it was difficult to find another school at short notice. All the good schools were full, they had waiting lists.

In the end my folks were desperate and they got me into Sapplewood. I don't think it had a great reputation."

Luke licked his lips and sipped some water.

"I don't remember any of this," she said.

"I went to Sapplewood." He picked up his glass and stared down at it, as if reluctant to go on. "Things didn't go well from the beginning." He kept his eyes on the glass, twisting it in his hands and swirling the water around. "It was very different from Chilton. I was miserable..." He said the last words in a whisper.

Kate's heart beat faster. She waited for him to go on.

"It was bad." He bit his lower lip, holding his breath as if in pain.

"You don't have to talk about this, it was a long time ago."

"No, I must." He exhaled and took a deep breath. "I had some sort of breakdown. I was ill... your parents came to fetch me." He frowned. "I thought you were in the car."

Suddenly Kate felt a spasm in her chest. A picture flashed into her mind. They were in the car; her father was driving. Luke was curled up in a ball on the back seat. He was wrapped in a red tartan blanket. She was in the front. He was crying and she kept turning around to look at him. Her mother had her arm round him. It was a long journey. It was dark when they got home.

"Yes, now I remember, I was in the car." Other images returned. "They went into the school and I was waiting outside in the car for a long time. Outside that building. That building like a Greek temple. She shuddered. "That's why I had that feeling."

He didn't seem to hear her. He was sitting up straight, staring into the distance.

"I was cold, so cold. I couldn't get warm."

"When we got home, you went to bed. You stayed in bed. There were phone calls. The grown-ups whispering. Then one morning you were gone, your parents came in the night to fetch you."

His eyes refocused on her.

"I don't want to talk about it anymore," he said in a flat voice, "there's no point. But when you said you were going there, to that place, it all came back."

She made coffee and they sat in silence for a while.

"Kate, I'd never tell you what to do, but do you have to go... to that place?"

"I've been staying there all week, that's where the pottery course was. And don't forget, it was a long time ago you were there. The school is completely different. Different people."

He sighed.

"I know, you're right. Of course, you're right. I'm being stupid.

Irrational. Let's talk about something else."

Although he made an effort, Luke wasn't himself. He half-heartedly suggested going out to a pub.

"You look exhausted. Go home and have a good night's sleep. Will I see you again before you go?"

"I'm not sure, there are a few things up in the air."

He hugged her tightly and kissed her on the cheek.

"Take care of yourself, Katie," he said softly. His eyes were like shuttered windows.

In spite of her words, Kate was worried about going back to Sapplewood, but there was no way to get out of it. The only thing was to work hard and stay for as short a time as possible. She must 'hit the ground running' on Monday. She'd planned to call a friend and meet her in the park on Sunday afternoon, but changed her mind. She could make a start on the Sapplewood project. There were things she could do before she went to the school; research other boys' boarding schools, look at their online presence, so she understood the competition.

As she lay in bed, almost asleep, Kate remembered something. She opened her eyes. It was when Luke was staying at her house when they'd brought him back from Sapplewood, and he was in bed. She hadn't heard most of the conversations and phone calls about him. Once though, a door had been left open and she'd heard her mother talking to Luke's father. She remembered the urgency in her mother's voice. And her words.

"But Phil, he keeps saying the boy died. And it was his fault."

Kate had never wondered before about what she'd overheard that night. It was clear the matter was a serious one. Why'd she never asked later on what had happened at Sapplewood? It was too late now. Her mother's sudden death had left a great many unanswered questions. Her father's over-hasty, ill-advised remarriage had strained their relationship, and his early retirement to Spain, had all but severed it. She couldn't ask him.

On Sunday, Kate put her doubts to the back of her mind. She was determined to find out as much as she could about boys' boarding schools in general and Sapplewood in particular. There was plenty of information on the Internet. She knew of Eton and Harrow but hadn't heard of any other establishments. She was surprised at how many parents were willing to send their sons away to school, and how many could afford to do so. After studying a number of websites and prospectuses, a pattern emerged. The schools looked like stately homes in the best British tradition. Mr Radcliffe had referred to Sapplewood as venerable, whereas it was relatively young, being founded in 1870, while others were many centuries older.

The website of every institution showed photogenic pupils wearing pristine shirts, dark blazers and perfectly knotted ties, looking both angelic and manly. These immaculate paragons performed activities from sports to scientific experiments to listening in class with expressions of rapt enjoyment on their faces. They sat on grassy banks reading and conversing with others in perpetual sunshine.

Dormitories with rows of narrow beds were a thing of the past. The study bedrooms wouldn't have looked out of place in a five-star hotel. And the food... her mouth watered at the menus thoughtfully provided, so parents needn't worry their precious offspring would be offered gruel. Gluten free, vegan, and all manner of options were available. And as far as the school facilities, vast indoor swimming pools, state of the art laboratories, award winning theatres, golf courses – the list was endless.

This was all very well, but what about the academic side? Several third parties provided comparison tables and ranking charts. The examination results were surprisingly varied. Many schools produced high achievers, but there were those whose results were disappointing.

After a crash course in the independent boys' boarding school sector, Kate focused on Sapplewood. She'd only seen the main building, pottery studio and part of the grounds, but with her newfound knowledge, she imagined many other exciting facilities were yet to be discovered.

She was wrong. She started with the current school website and prospectus. Sapplewood boasted cricket, rugby and football pitches, and a modest swimming pool but not much more. Pupils could study music, drama, science and technology, but not in exciting purpose-built cutting-edge facilities. The school chapel, with its splendid stained-glass windows, was the most impressive building – not an enticing attraction for modern day pupils. It'd be difficult to produce publicity material of a comparable standard to the other schools. How could Sapplewood's limited resources be presented in a suitably compelling form, even with her design skills?

She looked at the file of new, professional photographs. These were better. The photographer knew what he was doing, and the pictures were excellent. Appropriately dressed, delightful-looking pupils were portrayed performing the usual range of activities. The photographer had used clever camera angles and photographic effects. Wherever possible the pupils were captured in close up, while he'd cropped the backgrounds or rendered them in soft, subtle focus so the inferior nature of the school wasn't discernible. Kate stared at each photograph carefully. She noticed many shots featured the same half dozen particularly appealing pupils. Also, one teacher, a clean-cut, open-faced man, appeared in settings from the sports field to the library. She looked forward to meeting this handsome individual.

She sat back. It wasn't as bad as she thought. With the photos and some clever design, she could produce what the Radcliffe wanted. After packing up her laptop, camera and suitable smart clothing, she went to bed early.

Arriving at the school the next morning, Kate found quite a different scenario to the previous week. Rows of cars were parked outside the main building and navy-jacketed boys of all sizes were milling around in the lobby. She pushed her way through to Mr Radcliffe's office. Mrs Anderson, looking even more harried than before, was barely visible above the pile of paperwork on her desk. She looked up and glared at Kate.

"Good morning. I was wondering where I should go... where my room is?"

"What room?" the woman snapped.

"I'm staying here for a few days. Mr Radcliffe said I could stay in a... study bedroom."

Twin vertical lines appeared on Mrs Anderson's forehead.

"He never said anything to me about a room," she snorted, staring at Kate as if accusing her of lying. Mr Radcliffe's door opened and the head came out. At first, he looked surprised to see Kate, but quickly recovered.

"Miss, er, Fielding, good to see you. Mrs Anderson, will you make the necessary arrangements. Organise accommodation for our guest." He went back into his room without waiting for the secretary's response.

The woman sighed deeply.

"Wait outside," she said, "someone will come and get you." She picked up the phone.

Kate went out into the lobby, when suddenly a shrill bell rang . She jumped back in alarm. What was happening? The masses of boys immediately left the lobby. Of course, the school bell. She'd have to get used to that sound. She sat down in the now silent lobby. Half an hour later she was sure she'd been forgotten and wondered what to do next. She didn't fancy entering the lion's den again. Fortunately, a young woman in an apron came up to her.

"Miss Fielding? Please come with me."

They made their way through a bewildering maze of corridors, out of the back of the building, along a path until finally they reached a small building standing alone. Kate followed her guide inside and down another dark corridor. At the end, the young woman opened a door.

"Here you are, Miss Fielding," she said and left Kate standing in her new abode.

The Sapplewood prospectus hadn't included any images of the living accommodation, but she'd assumed it would be of a reasonable standard, even if not top class like other schools.

Once again, she was wrong, at least in this case. The room was dark – a mass of ivy growing up the building obscured the window. She turned on the light to reveal a sorry sight. A narrow bed stood against the wall, the wooden desk was scarred by generations of graffiti and the chair had a stained fabric seat. She sat on the bed which sagged beneath her. The stale air was stifling, even though the room was cold. She tried to open the window, but the pressure of the encroaching ivy was too great.

Kate decided to check out her neighbours and establish who else was living in the small building. She went along the corridor looking into each room. They were identical to her own, except they were dusty and the beds unmade. By the stairs she found a small kitchen. This also hadn't been cleaned recently and the fridge and cooker were disconnected. The two higher floors were the same.

She went back to her cheerless room, sat at the desk and switched on her laptop. No Wi-Fi. She'd have to find somewhere else to work. This was no hardship; the dismal atmosphere was oppressive. There must be a library. As she left the room, Kate turned to lock the door. There was a keyhole, but no key, no way of securing the room. That meant she could never leave anything of value there. She'd either have to carry things around with her or lock them in the boot of her car. Worse than that, at night she'd be vulnerable, alone in the building, some distance from the rest of the school. She must get a key.

Kate located the library in the main building, immediately feeling at ease. She loved libraries and this high-ceilinged room with its dark wooden shelves and parquet floor was a haven. She sat down and began to work. After an hour, she was in desperate need of coffee. But where to find it?

At the counter, a man with reddish hair and neatly trimmed beard was sorting books.

"Excuse me, is there anywhere I can get coffee?"

He looked at her.

"I presume you're staff?"

"Not exactly, but I'm working here for a few days... publicity."

He smiled.

"That counts as staff." He took a printed sheet from behind the counter, it was a plan of the school campus. "Here's the staff room, it's in this building on the next floor. You can get coffee there."

"Thanks, this'll be really useful. It's confusing. My name's Kate, Kate Fielding."

"Pleased to meet you Kate, I'm Hugh Davenport, the librarian. Let me know if I can help you in anyway."

This pleasant interchange, short as it was, raised her spirits. At least one person in this place was helpful.

Kate opened the staff room door and entered with some trepidation. It was a large bright room with desks and a photocopier. At one end there was a sink, fridge and kettle. She made herself a coffee and found an empty chair in an inconspicuous position. She drank the coffee and felt better. Realising no one was looking at her, she studied the other occupants of the staff room, noting the presence of a couple of female staff members. After another coffee, she stood up to go. On her way to the door, the school bell rang again. This time she was less startled by the sound.

Kate opened the door and stepped out. She walked towards the staircase and descended the first few steps. Then all hell broke loose. The bell had heralded the end of a lesson. The pupils were switching to other classrooms, like a herd of wild animals on the move. A horde of boys stormed the staircase, ignoring everything and everyone in their path. Kate clutched the banister tightly, expecting to be knocked to the ground and trampled. The noise of so many feet on the wooden steps was overwhelming. These were not even boys, they were men. She felt dizzy and shut her eyes. Bodies pushed past her, shouting and laughing as they thundered up the stairs.

"Kate, are you alright?"

The noise had receded and she opened her eyes. Adam stood next to her.

"I was a bit dizzy, silly of me. I'm okay now."

"You look pale, go down slowly."

She took one step at a time, holding onto the banister. He walked beside her.

"That herd of young elephants can be a bit much, especially on the stairs. Between lessons it's bad, but it's worse before lunch or at the end of the day."

"I'll remember to stay put when I hear the bell, thanks, I'm fine now."

"Okay. By the way, your mugs are dry and I'll be firing them tomorrow. Drop into the studio sometime and we can talk about glazes."

Back in the library, Kate had an idea. She asked Hugh, the librarian, if they had any books or publications about the school. He pointed out current and past editions of a magazine produced by students, as well as a book written about the school and its history by a former pupil. This included the school song, motto and crest. There were several other books that contained chapters about Sapplewood.

"You can take the books out of the library," Hugh said, "I'll give you a temporary ticket."

The school bell rang again and Kate looked at her watch, twelve fifty. Lunchtime. She couldn't face a dining room full of boys, but she was hungry. If only she could get away from the place. There must be a village where she could buy something. Google informed her there was a shop 1.8 miles away. Driving out of the iron gates, she breathed out in relief. Supplies at the village shop were limited, but she bought a couple of sausage rolls. While she sat in the car to eat them, her phone rang.

"Hello Kate, it's Henry. How are you doing?"

"Not too bad, it's good to hear from you."

"If you're not doing anything tonight, how about a drink?"

"I'd love to." she hesitated. "I know we said we wouldn't be eating out, but..."

"Is the school food that bad?"

"Not exactly..."

"Let's get a bite at the pub then. I'll meet you there at seven."

She sighed with relief. Another reprieve from the crowded dining room.

◆ ◆ ◆

Henry had already taken a table at the pub when Kate arrived. She smiled; it seemed an age since they'd last met. He gave her a searching look.

"How's it really going at the school? You can tell your Uncle Henry."

She sighed and did just that. When she described her expectations of the school from her online research, Henry shook his head.

"It's another world, private schools. You'd be shocked at the facilities at ordinary state schools nowadays. The lack of facilities, that is. Playing fields sold off, no investment in the buildings, antiquated equipment. Even Sapplewood is in another league. But of course, parents are paying."

She told him, with embarrassment, how frightened she'd felt when confronted by a mass of boys at close quarters. This time he nodded.

"That's the sort of thing I forget, I'm so used to being surrounded by groups of youngsters, and of course I'm much bigger than you."

"It sounds pathetic."

"No, under the circumstances it's quite understandable."

She didn't go into details about her room and the building where she was staying.

"That's enough about me," she said, "what about you? Have you found anywhere to live?"

"Not yet. I've been round some more estate agents and worked out exactly which villages would suit us. I've got viewings lined up for tomorrow."

They talked about Henry's property requirements for a while and then he asked how she was getting on with the job.

"I haven't achieved as much as I hoped. I need to find out more about the ethos of the school. Ways to show positive aspects of the student – I mean pupil – experience. To show why a boy would want to come to the school. Why a parent would send their son there. Any ideas, you're the education expert?"

He sat back and thought for a while.

"If I were you, I'd sit in on classes – all kinds of classes. Just sit at the back and watch and listen to the boys and the teachers. Sit in as many classes as you can, different subjects, different teachers."

"Would that be alright? Could I do that?"

"Didn't you say the headmaster said you could have full access? I'd use the school timetable. The timetables for each class should be on the school intranet. You can see the name of the teacher and location."

She nodded.

"Hugh, the librarian, will know all about that."

"Choose a class, go along early – before the bell – and ask the teacher, as a matter of courtesy, if you can sit in. They should agree."

Kate still frowned.

"I don't know, that sounds daunting."

Henry thought again. Then he slapped his leg.

"I know, why don't you start with Adam's classes? You know him, he knows you, you're interested in pottery. In short – Henry's genius plan."

She smiled.

"Well done genius. I can do that."

"There's something else, have you been to a school assembly?"

She shook her head.

"Do you think I should?"

"It'd give you a feel of the school – see the teachers and pupils all together."

"I could go in with Adam… Since you're on a roll, Henry, I've got another problem. I'm scared of the dining room; I haven't been in there yet."

"Why are you scared of that, what's scary about a dining room?"

"All those boys, pushing and shoving, noisy."

"Don't be silly; you'll eat in the staff dining room. Of course, you don't have to eat with the pupils. There'll be a dining room just for teachers and staff, quite separate. And not so noisy, not usually anyway."

Her face cleared.

"What an idiot I've been. I never thought of that. I could hug you."

He put on a frightened look.

"I'm a married man!" he squealed in a high-pitched voice and they both laughed.

"I feel so much better, you've solved all my problems. Thanks Henry."

"Glad to be of help. Good luck."

Kate returned reluctantly to her depressing room. She'd asked Mrs Anderson for a key a couple of times without success. It was icy cold, but there didn't appear to be any form of heating. She closed the curtains to shut out the menacing plant life outside and dragged the chest of drawers over to the door to prevent anyone entering in the night. She felt foolish, but safer. Wearing a sweater over her pyjamas, she got into bed and checked the emails on her phone before going to sleep. There was one from Fearne. It contained a newspaper article, dated two years earlier.

Tragedy strikes Sapplewood School

Max De Vere, a 16-year-old student at Sapplewood school died last Friday after falling from the bell tower of the school's chapel. According to headteacher, Giles Radcliffe, the incident was the tragic outcome of a schoolboy prank. An inquiry will be held, but no other students were involved and foul play is not suspected.

This tragedy follows a similar incident that occurred 26 years earlier. The school has a troubled history, with locals claiming it stands on ground cursed by unavenged deaths.

Shivering, Kate slid down in the bed, covering her face with the sheet. The image of the solitary schoolboy up in the bell tower in the dark filled her mind. Discussing the event with the others, it hadn't felt real. Only now, witnessing the scenario in her imagination, did she appreciate its true horror.

A barrage of questions shattered her indifference. She was filled with curiosity about Max's fate. She sat up in bed, wrapped in her coat, her brain fully alert.

How did Max die? Why? Was anyone else involved?

Logically there were only three possible answers to the first question. His death was either accidental, suicide, or he'd been killed by someone else. The other two questions were impossible to answer, she didn't have the necessary information. Could she find it? She was in the best place to do so – she had a unique opportunity to investigate. During her remaining time at Sapplewood, alongside her design work, she'd discover as much as she could.

Having made this decision, Kate lay down once more and fell into an uneasy sleep. She dreamed about Max. A vivid dream. He was standing in the bell tower, surrounded by deep blackness. An aura of light illuminated the boy's figure. The sadness in his eyes was heartrending, and his hands reached out to her in desperate supplication. He wanted her to uncover the truth.

CHAPTER 3

The next morning Kate woke up in a different frame of mind. The thoughts of the previous night and her dream seemed like the melodramatic results of an overactive imagination. She was no sleuth. Surely the police had investigated Max's death. With no experience or training, why should she do any better than them? While appreciating the real tragedy of the boy's fall, what hope had she of finding answers to her questions? Besides, she'd enough to do with the job she was being paid for.

She'd follow Henry's suggestions and have breakfast in the staff dining room. About to leave the bedroom, she hesitated. It might be intimidating even in the staff dining room, if she sat by herself and everyone looked at her. The book about Sapplewood's history and traditions she'd borrowed from the library lay on the desk. She could read it while she was eating, that'd give her something to do.

In the end, the staff dining room was bright and welcoming. As Kate helped herself to a substantial breakfast and sat down at an empty table, no one gave her a second glance. All the same, she looked at the book while she ate. Working her way through eggs, sausages, toast and fruit, Kate learned the school's motto.

If you plant a tree, knowledge grows. Si plantabis arborem scientiam.

The crest included an oak leaf, and the pupils were known as

Saplings. Following the arboreal theme, the four school houses were Oak, Ash, Cedar and Pine. There was even a school song, which she found quaint and a little absurd.

Grow, you fine young saplings
All planted in a line.
Grow, you fine young saplings
Oak, Cedar, Ash and Pine.

Drink, you thirsty saplings
When rain falls from the skies.
Drink you thirsty saplings
At the fountains of the wise.

Stand, you straight young saplings
Let roots and branches spread.
Stand, you straight young saplings
Throughout the years ahead.

Fight, you brave young saplings
And conquer when you must.
Fight, you brave young saplings
But let your cause be just.

Reach, you proud young saplings
For honour and for right.
Reach, you proud young saplings
For heaven's holy light.

Adam was alone in the studio when Kate arrived and he grinned at her.

"How're you getting on?"

"Fine thanks. I was wondering if I could sit in one of your classes today. I'm trying to get a feel of the school."

"No problem. I've got a nice group coming in at ten fifteen."

"That'd be great."

The pupils were first years. They enjoyed working with clay, no doubt a welcome change from more academic subjects. Adam showed them how to roll thin 'snakes' and then coil these round a small circular base to form a coil pot. The process was much more forgiving than throwing on the wheel, and by the end of the session all the boys had something to show for their efforts. Kate heard one of them say.

"Working with your hands gives your mind a chance to solve problems."

She thanked Adam.

"No problem. Do you fancy getting out of this place tonight and going for a drink?"

"Definitely," she said without hesitating.

Sitting in on a lesson had been a good idea. She'd spend the afternoon doing the same in other classes. Kate went to the staff room to check the timetables and plan her strategy. There she made a coffee and several members of staff nodded at her and smiled.

Back in the library, studying the websites of Sapplewood's competitors, she noticed they included short quotes from the pupils themselves. Whether these were actually said by the boys or made up, they came across well. She remembered what the boy had said in Adam's class, and decided to listen out for more. She'd intersperse these throughout the pages, as 'Sayings of the Saplings'.

Studying the various timetables, Kate selected a variety of classes to sample. The first she visited was English, waiting outside the classroom until the teacher arrived. He was a short, plump man with a handlebar moustache. His close-cropped hair was sprinkled with grey and he looked about fifty. A folded newspaper protruded from the pocket of his tweed jacket.

"Mr Dawkins?" she asked.

The teacher nodded.

"I'm Kate Fielding. The graphic designer. You've probably heard about me." Once again the nod. "I'm watching some classes to get a feel of the school. Would it be alright if I sat in on this one?"

Mr Dawkins tugged at his moustache.

"Don't see why not. Not very exciting though."

He told her where to sit. The boys, aged about twelve, filed in and stood by their seats until Mr Dawkins gave them permission to sit. He carried no textbook, or any other teaching material, but threw his newspaper onto the table. Was he jaded, going through the motions after too many years of teaching?

The boys sat quietly, looking expectantly at the teacher. Mr Dawkins picked up the newspaper and stood in front of his table.

"What's this?" he asked, unfolding the paper and holding it up. He nodded at the replies. "Which of you read a newspaper?"

Only one hand went up.

"So, Marshall, you read a newspaper?"

"No, sir, I just wanted to say that nobody reads newspapers anymore. It's all on the TV or Internet."

"Well, I do." said the teacher.

"Yes, but you're..." the boy burst out and then coloured. He stopped in confusion.

"Yes, Marshall, finish the sentence. You were going to say I'm … wise, amazing, extraordinary... That's what you meant isn't it?"

All the boys including Marshall laughed. Mr Dawkins continued.

"Be that as it may, today you're going to write a newspaper article. I'm sure you've all seen one." He held up the front page and went on to point out the headlines. "A good article should tell an interesting story about something important to its readers. Give me some headlines."

Hands were quickly raised and Mr Dawkins nodded at one boy.

"A spaceship landed in the middle of our rugby pitch and aliens abducted the players," was the suggestion. Expecting the boy to be reprimanded, Kate was surprised at the teacher's response.

"Excellent. Dramatic and important." He wrote the headline on the whiteboard.

"The price of chocolate goes down," was another suggestion.

"Of limited interest to the general public," Mr Dawkins said, but also wrote this one down. Soon an eclectic, imaginative list of headlines filled the board. "Now, exercise books out. Choose your headline and start brainstorming ideas. You've got the rest of the lesson to do that. Finish the article for prep."

The boy set to work with minimal disturbance as they jotted down ideas. Even then Mr Dawkins didn't sit, but walked round the class, noting what the boys were writing, commenting and offering help. When the bell rang, a few boys immediately closed their books and stood up, but the majority carried on writing. Mr Dawkins dismissed the class, folded his newspaper and replaced it in his pocket. He nodded to Kate on his way out.

"Thank you," she said sincerely, "such an interesting lesson."

Mr Dawkins tugged at his moustache and smiled.

"There's life in the old dog yet."

As Adam drove out of the school gates, Kate gave an involuntary sigh of relief. He looked at her.

"That's how I feel."

They left the village and drove to a pub Kate hadn't been to before.

"I wanted to get right away," he said.

"I thought you liked working at the school," she said when they were sitting with their drinks.

He grimaced.

"If you'd asked me that last week, I'd be careful what I said. But now I've got the contract... To be honest, I'm sorry I got you involved. Because I'm always short of cash, I think everyone else is. I thought it'd be a good idea."

"I don't understand, what's wrong with the school?"

"Where to start? For me it was the advert. They wanted an artist in residence. That sort of thing always sounds impressive. Looks good on the CV." He frowned. "It's my own fault. I didn't read the small print. They said I'd be working part time, just giving demonstrations. I'd have plenty of time for my own work. And I could use the facilities. The pay wasn't a lot, but they said I could run my courses in the studio.

"There was supposed to be a technician to prepare the clay and clear up. I'd have free accommodation and food. I could rent out my cottage – I've got a small place in Dorset. When I came for the interview, the school looked okay. I saw the grounds, studio and main building. The job sounded fine.

"But when I started..." he stopped. "Sorry, I'm talking too much. Do you want another drink?"

"Not yet, thanks, I'm really interested in what you're saying."

"When I got here, I wasn't doing demonstrations, I was teaching. Loads of hours. They said it was only temporary. They were getting another teacher. And there wasn't a technician, I ended up doing that job as well.

"When I got to know the others – members of staff – they put me straight. The school was only supposed to employ qualified teachers. And there's a pay scale. But an artist in residence was different. What they called a 'grey area'. The difference between a demonstration and a lesson wasn't clear. I was doing a teacher's job and technician's. And I only got a fraction of a teacher's pay."

"That's incredible, couldn't you do anything?"

"I tried and they kept promising. Radcliffe said he was doing what he could. It was only for a short time. Ended up being the same for a year."

"So why didn't you leave then?"

Adam shrugged.

"I'd kind of got used to it. I got a good rent for my cottage. I ran my courses three times a year. I made friends with other staff. They got someone to do a few hours helping out in the studio. It's hard to explain. You get stuck."

"Then what happened?"

"The second year started the same. Then they sent me on a course – out of the blue. First aid – residential – two days away. I couldn't understand it till I got back. The school inspectors had been here. Asking all kinds of questions. If they'd spoken to me, they'd have seen straightaway what was going on. The school was using an unqualified teacher. Radcliffe wanted me out of the way. After the inspection, things changed. Teachers left and weren't replaced. They cut corners. To save money.

"They said I'd have to pay them to run my courses in the studio. The cost would more or less cancel out my profit. In the end

I was going to leave. But while I was here, because of the long hours, I never had time to do my own work. I had no pots to sell. One gallery offered me a show. But I didn't have enough work or enough time to make more.

"Then out of the blue, this TV thing came up. When the contract was signed I gave in my notice. But I'm sorry about getting you involved."

"I don't see how it's going to hurt me. I'm working on the project; I'll have got what I need here in a few more days. I'll work on the rest of it at home and get paid."

He frowned.

"Don't give them anything without getting the money up front."

"Really? Do you think they won't pay me?"

"I wouldn't put it past them."

Adam went to the bar for more drinks.

"Sorry to go on about all this – the school and stuff. I just wanted you to know."

"No, it's fine. But if you don't mind since we're getting down to brass tacks, there are a couple of things I wanted to ask."

"No problem. Fire away."

"Why do people send their kids to Sapplewood? Surely, they must realise there're plenty of other schools? Are the fees lower or something?"

"Yeah, but the expenses are the same. I didn't know about any of this when I came. I heard it from other teachers. There are also foreign boys. From rich families. They want a British education. They pay more."

"Why don't they take more foreign boys then?"

"If there're too many – the place doesn't really feel British. If they pay through the nose to be in England, they don't want to be with a lot of other foreigners.

"They also give out a few scholarships to boys who would be a draw. Who would only come to the school with a scholarship."

"You mean they help boys who couldn't afford to come to the school otherwise? Help them to get a better education? Isn't that good?"

"I'm not talking about bright boys from state schools." He paused as if thinking. "This is how I understand it. There are a few families and boys, who are sort of 'influencers'. Radcliffe gives them a scholarship – what do they call it?" He frowned and then his brow cleared. "Honorarium. It's a kind of bribe to make them choose Sapplewood. Other families follow them. By giving out a bit of money, they get a whole group of other boys who pay the full price."

She sat back. It was hard to believe, yet it made sense from the school's point of view, if the headmaster was unscrupulous enough.

He went on.

"He also gets young teachers – straight out of college. They don't have enough experience. But they have to deal with difficult classes. Too many teaching hours. A young guy last year – a maths teacher – had a lot of issues with discipline. He got no support and, in the end, he had a breakdown and had to leave."

Kate sighed. The distasteful aspects of Sapplewood Adam mentioned, reminded her of Max's death. The desire to know more made her bold.

"The other thing I wanted to ask was about the boy who had the fall, who died."

Adam flinched.

"I know you don't want to talk about it, but the whole thing worries me," she said.

He looked down.

"It's difficult. Someone dying like that."

She leaned forward.

"You've told me there are lots of things wrong at the school, is there anything that could have led – contributed to Max's death?"

He looked at her sharply.

"You know his name?"

"Yes, Fearne sent me a newspaper article about it."

Adam drained his glass. He took a deep breath.

"The truth is, I don't know."

"Did you know him?"

"By sight. I never taught him. He was a good-looking boy – clever, good at sport. Not interested in pottery. He was one of those boys I was talking about. His dad was at the school, had connections. I heard Max got an honorarium."

"What about that night? Is it easy for the boys to get out of their rooms at night? Is there any kind of security?"

Kate thought of her own keyless room. She'd asked Mrs Anderson for a key several times, received vague replies, but no key.

"The head makes out the boys are tucked up in their own beds all night." He gave a hollow laugh. "That's not true. They're not prisoners. There're rules, but discipline in this school is – patchy. Everyone knows boys get out at night into the grounds – smoking, drinking – and meeting girls from the village."

He shrugged.

"For a while, after it happened, the head got one of the gardeners to patrol at night. But the guy only got a few quid extra and he was working all day. Most of the time he was asleep in a shed."

"I'm sorry to go on, but what do you think Max was doing up in the bell tower? Why was he there? Was he alone? Was he the sort of boy who drank?"

"I really don't know. This isn't a good idea. The police went into it all at the time..."

"Sorry. Let's talk about something else. Have you fired my mugs yet?"

Kate 's unanswered questions stuck in her mind. Adam might not know the answers, but there must be someone at the school who did. If only she could find them.

"Is this it?" Adam said as he drew up outside the building where Kate was staying.

"Yes."

"What's your room like? I thought this place wasn't being used."

"Not great, but it's only for a few days."

"Are you sure? It's a bit isolated."

"It's fine."

He didn't look convinced.

"Thanks for the evening," she said and got out of the car.

She returned to her uninviting room with a shudder. The air was cold and damp. Shivering she undressed quickly and put on a sweater. She dragged the heavy chest of drawers across the door and crept into bed. Curled up in a ball, she stiffened. What was that noise? Was someone outside her door? It sounded like a tap.

No, she'd imagined it. It was probably the wind blowing the ivy against the window. But there was no wind that night. And the sound came from the door. Another tap, louder this time. Kate lay in bed, rigid with fear. Who was it? What did they want? If she kept quiet, maybe they'd go away. She felt under the pillow for her phone. It wasn't there.

The noise grew louder. Her heart echoed the sound and the rhythm of the banging, her nerves jangling. She jumped. Was that her name? The sounds reverberated in the hallway. Did she hear "Kate! Kate!"? Yes, he knew her name. He was coming after her.

Her phone was on the desk, she must get it. She mustn't make a noise – then he'd know she was in there. She sat up and lowered her feet onto the floor. The room was completely dark. She had to reach the desk without tripping or banging into anything. She felt her way down to the foot of the bed, her bare feet making no sound on the floor.

Suddenly the banging stopped. Kate straightened and stood still. Was the door handle turning? It was impossible to see. The chest was sturdy, but would it keep the door shut? She forced herself to edge along the wall. At last, she came to the desk.

Abruptly the banging started again, her heart lurched and she nearly fell over. The phone. Concentrate on getting the phone. There was her handbag. With trembling fingers, sightless in the thick blackness, she searched every part of the bag. Nothing. She ran her hands frantically over the desk. The phone wasn't there.

Where else could it be? She'd never find it in the dark – but if she turned the light on – if whoever was outside saw it shining under the door... With a hammer blow to her heart, Kate remembered Max. If he'd been killed... was the killer still at the school? Terror took over. Would her lifeless body be found the next day?

But the banging stopped. The chest didn't move. Had the intruder given up? Gone away? Kate waited, hardly daring to breathe. Was the nightmare over? A chill rose up from the icy floor. Her hands and feet grew numb, but still, she didn't move. In the end, after it seemed hours had passed, stumbling on lifeless feet, she groped her way back to the bed. Under the covers, the blood returned to her hands and feet and she wrapped her arms round herself. She lay trembling until dawn finally broke.

◆ ◆ ◆

In the morning, the room looked cheerless and depressing, but no longer possessed the nightmare atmosphere of the previous night. But the banging had been real enough. She wouldn't spend another night without a key.

Kate entered the staff dining room for breakfast, and as she was carrying her tray to an empty table, Adam called her.

"Hey, you must've been out like a light last night. You left your phone in my car and I knocked on your door loud enough to wake the dead."

So, it'd been Adam last night – a simple explanation – not a scene from a horror film. She'd worked herself up into a state for nothing. It was him who'd called her name, not a murderous psychopath.

"I was awake, I heard you, but I don't have a key to the room. I pushed a chest of drawers across the door. If I'd known it was you…"

"That's no good. Why haven't you got a key?"

"I've asked Mrs Anderson, but—"

"That's a waste of time. I'll get onto Ned Hurst – he's the maintenance manager. I'll make sure you get it before tonight."

"Thanks so much."

"No problem."

"Come and join us," he continued, pulling out a chair. He pointed at the man beside him. "This is Bryan, he's Mr Music."

The fringe of the man's light brown hair fell across his face, and he continually pushed it away with long, sensitive fingers. Behind silver rimmed glasses his eyes were bloodshot. He gulped down coffee.

"Now I'm just about human," he said with a grimace, "Hello

Kate."

"What kind of music do you teach? I can't imagine most of the boys are interested in Mozart or Beethoven?"

A smile flickered across his face.

"You're right. I make a point of keeping up with current music that appeals to our pupils, they can relate to that. Apart from the odd boy who has a real interest in music or a real talent. Alas they are few and far between. Even then they mostly lack the dedication to practise."

Adam rose.

"My helper's not here today, got to go and get set up. I won't forget about the key, Kate." He nodded and left.

Bryan was staring into the distance.

"Occasionally a boy has talent and interest..."

"What happens to a boy like that? Do any go on to careers in music?"

"There was one boy, a couple of years ago. A talented pianist, and he could play the guitar as well. He was even composing, good music." He sighed. "He was one of those gifted individuals, outstanding at sport, very bright and all this came naturally to him. He didn't need to work hard. That's rare."

"What happened to him, what's he doing now?"

Bryan paused.

"He was... cut off. Before he had a chance to..."

Kate stared at him.

"What do you mean? What exactly happened to him?"

Again, Bryan paused and then spoke slowly.

"He died."

"Was that Max? Max De Vere?"

He nodded.

"I heard about him, and I wondered... Is it true he fell?"

"Yes. From the chapel. A terrible thing."

"Was it an accident?" She wondered if she was pushing Bryan, being too inquisitive, but he didn't seem to object.

"That's one theory."

"It wasn't, couldn't have been... suicide?"

A faraway look appeared on Bryan's face.

"There are more ways than one of committing suicide."

Suddenly he seemed to wake up and realise who he was talking to, and what he was saying.

"Don't take any notice of me, I've studied too many operas – too melodramatic. Max's death was an unfortunate accident."

Kate sat back in her seat. Here was someone who knew Max. Were Bryan's words just idle talk or did he know something about the boy's death as well?

Following Henry's suggestion, Kate entered the large school hall for the morning assembly. The room was full, the younger pupils sitting in neat rows on the floor, while the older boys and staff sat on wooden chairs. Apart from a low buzz of whispers, the room was peaceful and Kate didn't feel intimidated by the mass of boys. The noise died away as Mr Radcliffe swept into the room, his black gown billowing behind him. He strode on to the stage taking up a position in the centre. He waited until all the boys were standing. With his height and breadth, the headmaster cut an impressive figure.

"Good morning, Saplings," he said in a commanding voice.

"Good morning, Mr Radcliffe," was the reply. The head frowned. He was clearly not satisfied with the response. "That's a bit feeble. Let's try again," he said and then bellowed the greeting once more. "Good morning, Saplings!"

This time the boys yelled their response in an acceptable manner, and were instructed to sit.

Mr Radcliffe started by giving out information which meant little to Kate. She studied the pupils. She couldn't see individuals clearly, but the mass of youngsters sitting quietly, gave a pleasing impression. She looked at all the members of staff, remembering the good-looking male teacher she'd noticed in the new school photographs. She searched the rows of seated teachers, but he wasn't there.

Mr Radcliffe was now praising individual boys as well as sports teams for their achievements. He ended by a short speech of encouragement. While he spoke there was no whispering. He held the attention of the whole room, like a skilled actor, in his element on the stage. This was a different side of the headmaster.

"Let us all go out of here and make this our best day ever!" he said finally, with a sincerity and fervour that even stirred Kate.

After the assembly, Kate decided to hunt down the mystery man. Maybe Hugh the librarian would be able to help. When she went up to him, he was discussing with a pupil what to do about a lost library book. He smiled at Kate and made a gesture to show he'd be with her shortly. He quickly dispatched the boy.

"Good morning, what can I do for you?"

"Do you know where I can find a list of all teaching staff with their photos?"

"Yes, certainly, I have it. I'll give you the URL and password. Don't pass it on, please."

He handed her a slip of paper.

"Thanks, I'll burn this immediately after use."

He smiled and blushed.

She brought up the file on her laptop and scrolled through the thumbnail photos of the teachers. She didn't spot the target of her interest at first and repeated the process. Strange. She couldn't find him. After the third time, she was sure the handsome male teacher who showed up in so many of the official photographs was missing.

Encouraged by the success of Mr Dawkins' lesson, Kate arrived early for the next lesson she'd selected. The room was empty apart from a girl arranging papers on the teacher's desk. If she hadn't seen the girl in the staff room, Kate would've wondered what she was doing there. Miss Fiona Douglas must've been in her early twenties, but looked younger. Dark rimmed spectacles couldn't hide her pretty face with its pink rounded cheeks and full lips. Her severe suit revealed an attractive figure.

Kate explained who she was and what she wanted to the startled young woman.

"I suppose you can stay – did Mr Radcliffe say it's okay?"

"Yes, I'm sitting in on lots of classes to get a feel of the school."

Miss Douglas coloured and bit her lip.

"Alright, but this class, they're difficult." Her hands shook as she stacked the papers.

"I'll sit at the back and keep quiet," Kate said, "if that's alright.

The classroom door was wrenched open and suddenly the room was full of – men. That was the only way to describe the new occupants. Not more than fifteen in number, they dominated the space, making their presence felt, swaggering about the room as they selected their seats. Pushing chairs and desks and slamming bags and books, they talked loudly and broke out into laughter. Conscious of Miss Douglas' anxiety, youth and small stature, Kate's heart beat faster. Something felt wrong, an unequal balance of power in the room.

"Settle down, class," Miss Douglas said, and then cleared her throat. The noise in the room diminished but murmuring continued. The students lounged back in their seats; some had moved desks so they could cross their long legs in front of them. Ties were loosened and blazers draped over the backs of chairs. Kate felt sure this kind of behaviour wasn't permitted, it'd certainly not occurred in Mr Dawkins' lesson.

Miss Douglas carried on.

"I have the results of the test you did last week. We'll go through the answers. Pritchard, please give these out."

She held out the stack of papers. A boy with black curly hair sighed, stood up slowly and wandered towards her at a leisurely pace. He took the papers and also took his time giving them out. His classmates exchanged grins and talked to each other in low tones.

Miss Douglas stood by her desk.

"Come on Pritchard, we haven't got all day."

"I've got all day, I'm not in a hurry."

The voice belonged to another student, sitting near the front. He put his feet on a desk, and folded his arms. The others roared with laughter.

Finally, all the papers were distributed. Then began the painful task of going through each question. Miss Douglas read them out and asked for volunteers to give the correct answers. Her students used this as an opportunity to disrupt the activity. They asked her to repeat questions, interrupted her, made jokes and called across the room to each other.

Kate cowered in her seat, hoping not to be noticed and wishing she were a hundred miles away. The agonising exercise finally finished, Miss Douglas sat down at her desk and instructed the class to open their textbooks at a certain page. The boys made a performance out of this simple request. Pretending they couldn't find their books or deliberately dropping them, talking and laughing loudly all the while. Miss Douglas sat still, her face growing redder as she waited.

At last, a semblance of order returned. Miss Douglas asked a boy to read from the textbook. Unfortunately, he appeared to have a speech impediment, stammering and stumbling over the words so their meaning was lost. Kate felt mortified for the boy until he turned round to grin at someone behind him. He was faking. Fooling around. Miss Douglas stopped the boy.

"That's enough. I've changed my mind. We'll do something else."

The triumphant students whooped and catcalled, the noise loud enough to disturb any other classes in the vicinity, but nothing happened.

"I'm going to put some names up on the board, write them down."

The young teacher walked over to the whiteboard and picked up a marker, turning her back on the boys. Several of them stood up and walked over to other seats. Many put their feet on the desks. A particularly tall student, built like a rugby player, crept up behind the teacher. He tapped her on the shoulder and she swung round with a scream. This caused more merriment. One boy started a slow handclap.

In a shaking voice Miss Douglas ordered the boy next to her to sit down. He shook his head with an infuriating smile.

"Don't be so unfriendly, miss," he said, standing so close to her she couldn't get away. Some of his classmates came up to the front of the class to join him. Kate sensed a real danger in the situation. She must do something, but what? She stood up quietly, edged towards the door, opened it and ran out. She must get help. Now she understood why no one had been disturbed by the noise, the classroom was right at the end of a corridor, with no others in earshot. She ran to the nearest room and burst in.

"Please help, come quickly, Miss Douglas..."

Mr Dawkins was standing by the whiteboard. It took a while for her words to sink in. The young boys in his class whispered to each other.

"Everyone sit down. Get on with your work. I'll be back directly."

He followed Kate down the corridor without a word. Quite a different scene now met her eyes. The desks and chairs had been pushed back into neat rows, each boy was in his place, head bent over his textbook. No one made a sound. Miss Douglas sat at her desk, holding a tissue, her face blotchy. Her lips were pressed tightly together.

Mr Dawkins scrutinised the scene.

"Everything under control, Miss Douglas? Any problems?"

"No, no. We're fine. It's all okay," she said in a shaky voice.

"Nevertheless," said the English teacher looking at the boys through narrowed eyes, "it's almost time for the lunchbreak. I'll remain here until then."

When the bell rang, Mr Dawkins walked out of the room without a word. Kate followed him down the corridor.

"Mr Dawkins."

He stopped and turned to face her.

"I'm so sorry I troubled you, but when I left the classroom, I thought..."

He looked round.

"Are you heading for the dining room, Miss Fielding?"

She nodded.

"We can talk over lunch."

Sitting at a small table in a corner, out of earshot of the rest of the staff, Kate started again.

"I'm sorry, I really did think… the boys… They seemed to be out of control. I was afraid. I'm not used to this type of environment." She hung her head, avoiding his gaze.

"No need for apologies, I quite understand, and your instinct was sound. You were right to take action if you felt alarmed."

She looked up. Mr Dawkins tugged at his moustache.

"I'm aware of the situation. I'm sure the scene you left in the classroom wasn't the one I witnessed." He sighed. "Teaching requires a certain knack. No matter the age or sex or size of the pupils. Not everyone has it – and I'm not sure it can be taught. Some individuals who go into teaching find it's not for them. I've seen big, fierce looking teachers who fall to pieces when they face a lively class. Fortunately, I've never had a problem even when I first started. In spite of my relatively small stature and mild appearance." He smiled ruefully.

"I've never been afraid of my pupils, but more importantly, I treat all the boys as if they are decent and want to behave well – do the right thing. I expect the best from them, and usually get it. I respect them. I know they say respect should be earned, but I find the reverse can be true. Boys live up to the respect they are shown.

"Of course, they're not angels and don't always behave well in my classes, but by and large I've found most of the boys I've dealt with to be decent human beings."

"But the boys in Miss Douglas' class – they were menacing, I really thought she was in danger."

"I know the boys in question and believe me, Miss Fielding, it was just high spirits – showing off, you know, in front of a visitor."

"You mean me? I'm sure they didn't even realise I was in the room."

"Believe me, Miss Fielding, they were fully aware of your presence." He pulled on his moustache. "I must admit I have come across some wrong'uns – not many mind you. There've been a few boys who didn't respond well. There was one years ago – I wasn't surprised when he ended up in jail."

He shook his head.

"And there've been others. Someone else – even at a young age... There were alarming signs. Sadistic, psychopathic," He stopped, gazing into the distance as if remembering.

"What happened to that boy?" she asked, "how did he turn out?"

"We'll never know," he said.

They finished the meal in silence, then Kate spoke.

"Mr Dawkins, when did you start at the school?"

"A long time ago," he said with his rueful smile, "my debut is lost in the mists of time. No, the truth is I came to Sapplewood more than ten years ago."

"Wow, you must be the oldest – I mean the longest..."

"Longest serving member of staff," he finished her sentence. "I'm not sure. I've been here longer than most people. Apart from Pat Anderson, of course, she arrived the same time as me."

"Really? Mrs Anderson's been here all that time?"

"Yes. She came with her husband, who was a teacher."

"I don't remember seeing his name on the list of staff, what subject does he teach?"

He fingered his moustache.

"He's not here anymore. I'm afraid they separated – he left about five years ago." He looked at his watch. "I'd better be going. You're welcome to sit in on any of my classes, Miss Fielding, if that helps. Good day to you."

In spite of Mr Dawkins' words, Kate felt unnerved by the situation in Miss Douglas' classroom. Unsatisfied by his answers. She took a few deep breaths. Why couldn't he see? The boys weren't psychopaths but they were bullies - goodness knows how Miss Douglas coped with them if they always behaved like that.

Kate had a strong desire to get away from boys and teachers, but where to go? Not to her miserable bedroom or the staff room. In the end she went to the library, there at least the pupils were under control. Hugh smiled and nodded as she came in. Although she turned on her laptop, she didn't see the screen. Unable to concentrate, her whole being revolted against attending any more lessons. She'd seen enough. She wasn't surprised to find bullying at the school, but never expected to witness pupils bullying a teacher. Thoughts of bullying reminded Kate of Max, the boy who'd fallen to his death. Was he being bullied? The taunting, threatening pack of boys she'd seen earlier, they could've turned on a fellow pupil as they'd turned on Miss Douglas.

To take her mind off what'd happened, Kate looked through the photographs for the new version of the school website and prospectus. Were there enough to convey everything she wanted? If necessary, she could supplement these professional photographs with some of her own, which was why she'd brought her camera. Now she was familiar with the school, she viewed the pictures in a different light, and recognised most of the locations. She decided some photos of areas not included in the official pictures might be useful for her work. Once she left the school, she would've lost the chance to take them. Besides, she wanted to get outside. She collected her camera and set off.

It was a sunny day and the school buildings and grounds looked their best. Kate had no intention of photographing the same subjects as the professional photographer. He'd captured the main buildings and areas of interest in a highly successful manner. She was looking for quirky corners, unexpected sights and unlikely but attractive juxtapositions.

There was no point in snapping any of the boys – their everyday uniforms and untidy hair would make an unwelcome contrast to the carefully groomed images in the official photographs. She wandered around, taking a great many pictures and hoping a few might be suitable.

Entering the woods for the first time her spirits lifted. She remembered walking through other sun-dappled woods when swathes of bluebells covered the ground. It'd been a family tradition when she was growing up, longed for and enjoyed every year. Even as a child, the masses of delicately tinted flowers on the forest floor thrilled her soul. It was best when Luke came with. She smiled. They'd introduced him to the experience, but he was more interested in climbing trees than gazing at flowers. He'd shin up effortlessly and perch on a high branch.

"It's easy," he called, and waved, "look no hands!"

"Be careful, you'll fall," her mum cried.

"Not him," said her dad, "he's a born monkey."

Sometimes Luke would call down for Kate to join him.

"Don't you dare!" was her mum's immediate response, "it's much too dangerous for a girl."

How Luke loved England. Why did he choose a job that kept him away so much? And in such contrasting climates. Not for the first time, she wondered why he'd never married, or settled down with a partner. He'd sometimes mentioned women he'd met, but none of these relationships had endured beyond the end of the trip.

Kate could ask the same question about herself. She looked back on the most serious relationship in her life so far. She and David had been together for months and had moved in together. Things seemed to be going well. Luke had been away on an extended trip at the time, so hadn't met David until they were an established couple. It was just before Luke returned, that David proposed. Kate wanted time to consider this big step, so they told no one. Then Luke came back and they made plans for their usual Saturday get together. David assumed as her partner he would be included, but she didn't agree.

"We're such old friends – we've got so much to catch up on – you'd be bored."

With the benefit of hindsight, she recognised this had been an excuse. David's presence would spoil her precious time with Luke. David never gave her an ultimatum, but if he had, she would've chosen a day with Luke, over a lifetime with him. After that realisation, the relationship hadn't been the same and they parted a short while later.

When Kate told Luke she'd broken up with David, he hugged her tightly without a word. When his arms finally relaxed their hold, he took her by the shoulders, looking deep into her eyes as if reaching into her soul. She responded, meeting his gaze without reserve, but as she stared, strengthening the connection from her side, the shutters dropped down once more over his eyes, and biting his lip, he looked away. For so many years she'd wondered, did he really care for her? Or was she just like a sister to him? This was the test. His chance to show her his true feelings. To act. But he didn't.

In the sunshine the Sapplewood trees were at their best. *These woods must be older than the school buildings,* Kate thought, stroking the trunk of a venerable oak. Sapplewood – trees, Saplings.... she had an idea for her project. She'd lay down faint images of trees behind the text on some pages of the website. The effect would be subtle, unusual and suitable for the school's arboreal theme. She spent the next hour in the woods, photographing trees of every kind from different angles.

Meandering between the trees in the dappled sunlight, camera in hand, Kate was back in her childhood when she believed in fairies and expected to find them in the woods. She came across a charming sight. At first glance, it was a quaint, rustic cabin, surrounded by plants. *The home of a fairy or a good witch,* thought Kate the child. Then the adult took over. It was just a decaying wooden shed. Nevertheless, she took a number of shots, trying to capture the whimsical, magical feel of the place. In the middle of that sun-kissed dell, a cloud passed over the sun. The shed suddenly seemed menacing. She shivered. But the shadow passed and the scene was idyllic once more.

At the edge of the wood, on her way back, Kate saw a man splitting logs with an axe. He was dressed in muddy jeans and a worn khaki sweater. He stood up and as she saw his face, she gasped. In spite of the unkempt hair and stubble on his face, she recognised the mystery man – the much-photographed teacher who'd proved so elusive. Even in his current ungroomed state, he was extremely attractive. Perhaps all the more so. She gaped at him.

"Hello," she stammered.

The man looked blank. She recovered and smiled at him.

"I recognise you from the school photos. I haven't bumped into you before." She held out her hand, "Kate Fielding, I'm the graphic designer."

The man's expression didn't change. He regarded her with an unblinking, incurious stare, his arms hanging loosely by his sides. What was the matter with him? She made one more effort.

"I'm sorry I don't know your name, Mr?"

The man ignored her words, raised his eyes and looked over her shoulder. She heard the clumping of boots behind her.

"What's going on? What are you doing?" A thickset man with an unnaturally red complexion and bushy eyebrows glared at her.

"Who are you and why are you bothering my staff? What do you want?" His voice was harsh.

Kate stood back.

"I was just talking to this gentleman…"

"Gentleman, huh, that's rich. Get back to work, Glen. I told you to finish those jobs before eleven. Have you done them?"

The silent woodcutter hung his head and ambled into the wood.

"He's easily distracted," said the other man, "then he'll forget what he's supposed to do."

"I thought he was a teacher," Kate said, "I saw him in some photographs."

"Well, he isn't. He just helps out with odd jobs. Best to leave him alone." He stomped off.

What was the matter with the man? If the woodcutter was a teacher, as portrayed in the photographs, why did the thickset man contradict this? Kate was pondering the conundrum when her phone rang. She didn't recognise the number.

"Hello," said a female voice, "Miss Fielding? This is Mrs Anderson. Mr Radcliffe wants to see you as soon as possible."

She frowned at the woman's graceless manner and couldn't avoid a flicker of apprehension. Summoned to see the headmaster, what'd she done wrong? Ridiculous. She wasn't a naughty schoolgirl.

As she entered the headmaster's office, Mr Radcliffe invited her to sit down and Kate experienced deja vu as Mrs Anderson slammed down a tray with two cups of coffee in front of them.

"Thank you so much for coming so promptly, Miss Fielding. How are you getting on with our little project?"

"Quite well. I have a lot of material and ideas. If you'd like to see them, I'll get my laptop."

"No, no, I trust you entirely. I am sure your work will be… I will only need to see the finished product, which I'm sure will be excellent.

"It's about something else that I wish to speak to you." He sipped his coffee. "I've been told you're quite a photographer, Miss Fielding."

"How... who said that?"

"My dear Miss Fielding, in a closed community like this, the grapevine you know, is always active. I see you have a very fine camera. I wanted to ask you a favour, we have a small problem. On Thursday afternoon, a ceremony will take place at the school. A charitable organisation, the Weybridge Trust – you may've heard of it?"

She shook her head.

"No matter. This organisation raises money to help boys from – less affluent background – boys who would benefit from an independent school education, to do so. At this time, I am delighted to say they've chosen Sapplewood to work with. Together we've identified two worthwhile boys from the state sector – high achieving boys with great potential – to attend our school. As I said, the Trust raises money and, on our part, we offer substantially reduced fees.

"So, tomorrow, the ceremony will take place to present the awards to the recipients and acknowledge the contributions of both parties. This in itself is important, but we've just heard that our local MP has requested, er, has been invited to attend and make a speech. A photo opportunity, I believe it is called."

Kate wondered what all this had to do with her.

"As the name suggests, a photo opportunity requires a photographer. We've contacted the professional who took those excellent photographs for the rebranding exercise, but he's unfortunately unavailable at such short notice. Learning of your prowess with the camera, I wondered if you could help us out and photograph the ceremony?"

"Mr Radcliffe, I have a good camera, but I'm certainly not a professional, I really don't think—"

"I quite understand, but I urge you, Miss Fielding, to consider how useful these pictures would be to our website. By the way, I neglected to mention, our local MP is Jeremy Warren."

She considered this. Jeremy Warren, a short man with a distinctive mane of blond hair, was an up-and-coming young politician. He was expected to be offered a cabinet position in the near future, and some even tipped him as a potential Prime Minister. This changed the situation. Photos of him would definitely enhance the school's image. Also, she was intrigued to see the man at close quarters. But it would mean staying on at the school, she couldn't leave till Thursday night or Friday morning.

"What do you say, Miss Fielding? Will you come to our aid?"

"Alright, I'll do it, but only on the understanding that I am not a professional photographer and I can't guarantee—"

"Yes, yes, quite so." He waved away her objections.

Returning to the lobby, deep in thought about this assignment, Kate cannoned into someone. It was Adam.

"Hey, steady on," he said, "I've been looking out for you. How're you getting on?"

She stared at him, gathering her thoughts.

"Sorry," she said, "too busy thinking."

"Do you fancy going to the pub this evening?" he asked.

"Yes," she said, glad of the chance to get away.

CHAPTER 4

"**W**hat were you thinking about so deeply?" Adam said as they drove to the pub.

Kate told him about the headmaster's request and asked if he'd be at the ceremony. He shook his head.

"It's not my kind of thing. Everyone's supposed to go, but they won't miss me. That kind of formal event – it's not me. I'm just a simple potter. I didn't do so well at school. Luckily, I got into pottery through my stepdad. I was a sort of apprentice to him. That's how I learnt. My brother was the clever one in the family."

Adam's expression hardened. He went on, as if speaking to himself.

"He'd have a degree, a good job… What a waste."

"Don't you want to see the great Jeremy Warren in action?" Kate asked, trying to lighten the mood. "When you start doing the TV show you'll become a celebrity and people will be all over you."

"I don't like the dressing up. The other teachers have all been to university and wear their black gowns and stuff. Compared to them I look like the gardener."

His words reminded Kate of something.

"Oh, Adam, the strangest thing. I'm working with photographs of the school – buildings, pupils and teachers. The professional photographer took the pictures and there's one guy who's in a lot of them. He looks like a teacher, you know, tweed jacket, smart trousers and so on. I thought it was strange, he was all over the place, in classrooms, labs, sports pitches. I haven't seen him anywhere around, but today, I saw him in the woods, cutting up logs with an axe.

"I tried to talk to him, but he was weird. Then another guy came along and shouted at him. He called him Glen and said he was an odd job man. Do you know anything about him?"

By this time, they'd arrived at the pub. Bryan, the music teacher, was sitting on a stool at the bar. He was staring into his drink and didn't notice them. Adam went over to a table in the far corner.

"I hope he doesn't see us – he's already well away." He shook his head, "He's been overdoing it recently. There's a limit to what the headmaster will stand.

"You asked about Glen, yes, I know him. He does all kinds of jobs around the place, gardening, general labouring."

"But why would he be dressed like a teacher?"

He shrugged.

"I've never seen him in decent clothes. He always wears a mouldy sweater."

"And who's his boss – the guy who shouted at him?"

"That must be Ned – Ned Hurst – he's head of maintenance, buildings and grounds."

Kate sighed.

"I'm not happy about taking photos at the ceremony. What happens if I mess up? I don't know what they want. I wish the professional photographer had been available."

His brow furrowed.

"Why wasn't he?"

"Mr Radcliffe said they didn't find out till late and he had something else on."

Adam snorted.

"More likely they didn't pay him for the last job. Or they could get you cheaper."

He realised what he'd said. "Sorry, I didn't mean it like that. You'll be great."

At that moment there was a disturbance at the bar and they both turned. Swaying on his stool, Bryan was shouting and banging his glass on the bar. Adam and Kate stood up and as they watched, Bryan lost his balance and fell heavily onto the floor. As he fell, his glasses bounced on the stone floor, the lenses splintering. He didn't move.

The barmaid stood gaping with a half-filled glass in her hand, and the landlord came from behind the bar. Adam and Kate ran over.

"Are you alright?" said the landlord.

The prostrate man groaned. At least he was alive.

"My glasses!" he wailed.

Together with Adam, the landlord hauled him up into a chair, where he flopped, his head lolling.

"Now then, mate, I told you not to take that last pint." He turned to Adam, "Next time I'll stop serving him."

Adam nodded, "He's getting worse. I'll have to get him home." He turned to Kate. "I'll be back soon; he lives in the village."

"I'll come with you. You might need help."

"If you're sure – you don't have to."

Either side of the music teacher, they half dragged him to the car and manoeuvred him into the back.

"I'll sit next to him," she said, "just in case."

After a few minutes, Adam stopped the car outside a small

cottage. He got out.

"Hang on a moment."

By the light of a streetlamp, she saw him lift a plant pot and take something from underneath. He walked over to the front door and opened it.

They almost carried the inebriated music teacher inside and deposited him onto a grubby couch. The room smelt sour and on the coffee table lay a plate streaked with congealed fat. Crumbs dotted the plain carpet.

"He's too far gone to get up the stairs. A dead weight." Adam shook his head. "He's not usually as bad as this."

"My glasses, where're my glasses?" Bryan tried to get up.

"They're broken. Look." Adam held out the sorry spectacles.

Bryan put his head in his hands.

"Have you got a spare pair?" Kate asked, and he looked up.

"Yes."

"Where are they?"

He looked vaguely round the room.

"Upstairs," he said doubtfully.

Adam sighed. "I'll go and have a look."

Kate picked up the dirty plate and took it into the adjoining kitchen. The worktop was piled with crockery, cutlery and pans in a similar state. She dumped them in the sink and turned on the tap.

"What's going on? What're you doing," Bryan called from the next room.

"Just washing up."

"Leave my stuff alone! Don't touch my things!"

She turned off the tap and left the room.

"Where's Adam gone?" Bryan said.

"Upstairs, to look for your spare glasses."

He scowled. "They're not upstairs. Here, in that drawer." He pointed to a small wooden cabinet.

"Which drawer?" she asked, but Bryan's head was in his hands and he didn't seem to hear.

She opened the top drawer which contained pens, pencils, glue and a collection of keys, then tried the next one.

"What're you doing? Stop that!"

Bryan's yell made Kate jump and she slammed the drawer shut. But not before she'd seen something.

Adam came back into the room.

"I've found your glasses, d'you want to put them on now?"

Bryan snatched the spectacles.

"She's going through my stuff. I don't want her here," he said glowering at Kate.

"Alright, no problem, we're going. Will you be okay now?"

"Yes. Get her out of here."

"I'm sorry," Adam said as he drove back to the pub, "thanks for coming. I hope the evening's not totally ruined."

"No, it's okay. I was only looking through his stuff because he said his glasses were there, I wasn't snooping."

"Of course not. He's just in that paranoid stage."

"But I saw something, in the drawer."

"What was it?"

"A gun."

The car swerved.

"What did you say?"

"A gun. I saw a gun in his drawer."

"A real gun – you mean like a revolver?"

"I think so. I don't know about guns."

"Why would Bryan have a gun?"

"You don't think – if he's depressed – he might, you know...?"

He shook his head.

"No, I'm sure he wouldn't."

"Shouldn't we – take it? Not leave it there."

"No, he'll be alright. He'll sleep it off and be back at work tomorrow."

They said no more until they reached the pub. Adam kept the engine running.

"You're right. I can't leave the gun there. You go in and I'll nip back and get it. Just to be sure."

Back at the pub, Kate went to the Ladies'. The girl from the bar was washing her hands. She looked at Kate and muttered, "Bastard."

"I'm sorry?" Kate said sharply.

The girl went on.

"Him. That drunk guy. Bryan," she said with a sneer, "you were here that day when they were talking about the accident at the school," she added in a low voice.

"Yes," said Kate, "has he got something to do with—"

"Not in here," the girl hissed, "come out the back. I'm just taking five, Dad," she called to the landlord.

Kate followed her to the dark yard behind the building. The girl lit a cigarette, its tip glowing in the dark. She drew on it a couple of times and then spoke.

"I know I shouldn't talk about it – specially to a stranger. Well maybe a stranger's better. I can't talk to anyone else round here. It's about Max, the boy that died."

"Did you know him?" Kate asked.

"Yes, we were – together. But nobody else knew. It was a secret. Mum and Dad would've killed me... We weren't supposed to mix with the boys from the school and Mum works there."

"How did you get to know him?"

"I used to do cleaning at the school. We got talking one day. He was so good looking." She paused as if remembering.

Kate couldn't see her face properly in the dark, just the red tip of her cigarette.

"I was sixteen, so was he. He was my first boyfriend and he told me he hadn't had a girlfriend before. I was surprised, a boy like that. We used to meet in the woods at night. There's a kind of hut."

Now that the girl had started, the words flooded out in a rapid stream.

"It was you know – romantic. Like I said, I would've got in a lot of trouble, but we were in love. We were going to be together when we finished school. No one could stop us then." The flow of words stopped.

"What's your name?" Kate asked.

"Tara."

"Well Tara, how did that guy – Bryan – come into it?"

"I'm getting to that. Max was very good looking. And he was good at school, everything. He was very good at music. That guy," she spat out the words, "he's the music teacher. He had a thing for Max. Max thought it was funny, a man like that keen on him. He told me all the things the guy said. He used to imitate him. The teacher wrote a song about him, Max said it was the best joke ever. He showed me. I didn't like it. It was pathetic. I thought he should tell Bryan he wasn't interested or report him. But he wanted to string him along, for fun.

"Then the man wanted to meet him at night, I got really annoyed. Max said I was jealous. I wasn't jealous, it was sick. He's a pervert. Max was laughing, he said he could get the guy fired. We had a big row. And then..." her voice shook. "I didn't see him again... I never saw Max again.

"When they said he died at night, I just knew it was something to do with the guy. They must've met. Maybe Max laughed at him and the guy got angry and pushed him."

Now she was crying, her hands covering her face. The cigarette had fallen to the ground. "He killed him. I know he did. He killed Max."

"Oi, what are you up to out here? Tara, you're needed in the bar."

"Alright Dad," the girl murmured sniffing, and went inside.

When Kate returned to her seat, Adam was back.

"Did you get it?"

He nodded.

"What're you going to do with it?"

"Hand it into the police. I'll be glad to get rid of it."

"Where could he have got it?"

"No idea. The school has a cadet force – but I thought they only used rifles, and I'm sure they're locked up."

Thank goodness Adam had taken her seriously and gone back for the gun. Bryan was in a bad way – who could tell what he would do. Why was he in such a state? Max had died two years ago; did they really have a deep relationship? Tara didn't think so, but perhaps she was wrong. Maybe she was right about his involvement in Max's death, though. If Bryan had accidentally caused the death of the boy he loved... It would explain a lot.

◆ ◆ ◆

The awards ceremony was to take place at five on the Thursday afternoon. Kate couldn't focus on anything else all day. She checked again and again that her spare camera batteries were charged. She started different tasks, but her thoughts returned to the forthcoming event. She was sure to make a fool of herself – in front of the whole school.

She went in and out of the staff room, drinking cup after cup of coffee. She now felt quite at home there and greeted or smiled at other staff members. One time the room was empty, apart from two young women. As Kate sipped her drink, a loud expletive startled her.

"This computer is completely rubbish. It's driving me mad!" said one of the teachers.

"You'll have to give in and buy your own laptop like me," said the other.

"Why should I? The school should provide proper equipment for us to do our jobs. This thing is an antique."

"They're all the same. A couple of years ago one of the boys persuaded his dad to replace the whole system – all the computers. He was loaded – had his own software company. We were going to get top of the range Macs."

"What happened?"

"It was Mrs Anderson. She stuck her oar in. Made a big fuss, said she wanted to keep her machine. But the deal was to replace the whole system or none."

"But why on earth...?"

"I heard she couldn't cope – didn't want to learn a new system."

"Pathetic. I'm surprised Radcliffe didn't get rid of her."

"He'd never get someone else to do her job for what he pays her."

The speakers, who'd been talking loudly, noticed Kate for the first time and the conversation ended abruptly.

Kate put on her smartest outfit and was the first in the assembly hall, taking the opportunity to try out camera angles. All the action would be on the stage and she stood in different spots, even climbing onto the stage, to find the best vantage points. Then the boys trooped in and she moved away.

At a quarter to five, the boys and staff were all seated. Adam was nowhere to be seen, but as he'd predicted, all the teachers were wearing black academic gowns and hoods in colours that indicated the institute and department of their degree. The boys also made a better show than usual.

Mr Radcliffe entered the hall, and climbed onto the stage, where six chairs were arranged, along with a standing microphone. He tested it and looked round with a satisfied smile. He left the stage and hurried out of the hall. Everyone waited, initially in silence, but as the time went by, murmuring broke out in all parts of the room.

A short while later, a beaming Mr Radcliffe ushered in two embarrassed looking boys – presumably, the recipients of the awards – and their parents – followed by another man and woman. The parents were given seats in the front row, while the others mounted the stage. There was one empty seat for Jeremy Warren. Everyone rose.

Kate wondered whether she should get in a few shots, but her nerve failed her. After a while Mr Radcliffe motioned for the boys to resume their seats. Nobody seemed to know what to do next, apart from the head, who radiated confidence and authority. The others on the stage were clearly ill at ease. The two boys stared at the ground, one shuffled his feet and twirled a lock of hair around his finger while the other slouched back in his chair, sitting up every so often with a jerk.

Someone came in and stood in the doorway. The audience looked over expectantly, but it wasn't the well-known politician, it was Mrs Anderson, an agitated Mrs Anderson. She scuttled to the stage, her hair escaping from its bun and her glasses on their chain bouncing as she went. She climbed the few steps onto the stage and said something to Mr Radcliffe. He nodded and held up his hand for silence.

"I have just received notice that our guest of honour, Mr Jeremy Warren, has been delayed – no doubt on important business – but he is on his way and will be with us shortly."

He smiled beatifically and sat down with a flourish of his black gown. The minutes ticked by and inevitably the boys grew restless. They started with whispers, but the volume soon increased. Finally, Mr Radcliffe rose once more.

"Gentlemen, I am sure Mr Warren is not keeping us longer than is absolutely necessary. Please have the courtesy to remain silent."

As he finished speaking, there was a commotion at the entrance and the audience turned round. As the door was being held open by a dark suited minion, the well-known figure of Jeremy Warren made his entrance. His blond hair gleamed, but he was shorter than he appeared on TV. He stood still while the boys rose, and waited until he had the full attention of the room. Then he strode confidently to the front, smiling and waving.

The boys broke out into spontaneous applause. The politician made his way to the stage and mounted it, by which time Mr Radcliffe was ready to greet him. The two men shook hands and Mr Radcliffe directed Mr Warren to the remaining seat. However, whether he didn't notice – or didn't want to relinquish his position – the MP ignored the gesture and remained standing centre stage.

"I would like to welcome our visitors," Mr Radcliffe gestured to the man and woman on the stage, "our friends from the Weybridge Educational trust. The two fortunate recipients of the awards," he pointed at the squirming boys, "and of course our guest of honour, the man who has served our local community so ably for the last five years, our member of parliament, Mr Jeremy Warren."

At this Jeremy waved once more as if he were royalty. He took control of the microphone, almost pushing the taller man out of his way.

"Thank you, headmaster for that warm welcome. And now let us begin."

With no other option, Mr Radcliffe sat down. Standing at the side of the hall, Kate was overwhelmed by the politician's grand entrance. She looked at the camera in her hand as if she was wondering what it was doing there. When she realised, it was with a gulp. How could she dare? She couldn't possibly approach the stage. She took a few shots from where she was standing. At least that was a start.

On stage Jeremy Warren was in full flow.

"Good afternoon, Saplings!" he cried.

"Good afternoon, Mr Warren," came the thunderous response. He waited for it to die down.

"Or should I say, my fellow Saplings. As you all know I too was a Sapling. But I'm sure everyone in this room will agree, once a Sapling always a Sapling." The last words were spoken in rousing tones. Yet again, the applause was lengthy.

"Education, I strongly believe is one of the cornerstones of a civilised society. As I say, I was fortunate enough to receive an excellent education, both here and at those other institutions of learning. Sir Bertram Weybridge was of the same mind. A man of lowly birth and straitened means, who had the opportunity – through the generosity of a benefactor – to receive a good education. He believed that he achieved his position, as the founder of a highly successful business, as a result of this education, and he wanted to pass it on to others, through the educational trust he created."

Kate now urgently felt she should be taking pictures. As inconspicuously as possible, she worked her way to the front and took some shots. She checked the images. These were better, but if only she could get closer. Mr Warren was still talking.

"I also attribute a good deal of my success to my education. Some people say I've made remarkable progress at my relatively young age. Of course, in all modesty, I can't deny some natural talent..." He stopped and his audience laughed as he meant them to.

At this point, Kate reached the stage, keeping low to escape attention. As he registered the audience's reactions, Jeremy Warren spotted her and raised one hand.

"Excuse me, I believe I see someone I've failed to greet. The photographer who's recording this important event. Please stand up, madam."

Her face burning, Kate ignored his words and crouched down to escape notice. But this wasn't permitted. Everyone looked at her and Mr Warren continued with encouraging smile.

"Don't be bashful. Please show yourself."

Kate had no alternative and in an agony of embarrassment, she stood up, her head hanging. Mr Warren continued the torture, by clapping.

"Well done. Bravo. Now please continue your work, we'll hinder you no longer. By the way, this is my best side." Once again ripples of laughter spread through the rows of boys.

There was nothing for it, either she slunk away, her tail between her legs, or she went on with her job. Not giving herself time to think, she focused her camera on the MP and the other occupants of the stage, as if they were images and shapes, not people. As if she were back in the woods, alone, photographing trees. The rest of the room was just background. Mr Warren continued to talk, but Kate heard nothing. Luckily, the audience lost interest in her, and she moved around silently, all her design instincts to the fore, composing, zooming in and out.

The two scholarship boys were introduced and ceremonially handed certificates by the MP, who stood between them. He knew how to maximise the potential of such a situation. He was constantly centre stage, shamelessly blocking others so he could dominate the scene and the photographs.

Before Kate realised, the ceremony was ending. Everyone sang the school song with gusto and soon Mr Radcliffe was shaking hands with Mr Warren and the party vacated the stage.

She stood up and exhaled. The boys filed out, giving her curious glances as they went. It was over. Her legs shook and she sat down, head dizzy with images. She was too tired to drive back home that night and she couldn't face the staff dining room. She must get out.

Kate rang Henry and he agreed to meet her at the pub.

He'd eaten earlier, but as he watched Kate demolish steak and kidney pie and mash, he frowned.

"You look all in, what's been going on?"

She told him about the ceremony and he raised his eyebrows at the mention of Jeremy Warren.

"Smarmy so and so," was his opinion.

Before she could reply her phone rang. It wasn't clear who was on the other end of the call and Kate made a series of short comments, her expression changing as she spoke.

"Come on, tell Uncle Henry all, that's a terrible phone call to listen to for a nosy parker like me. Spill the beans. Who was it?"

Kate bit her lip.

"Actually, it was someone called Tris, apparently he's Jeremy Warren's personal assistant."

Henry's eyes opened wide.

"What does the great man want with you?"

"I'm not exactly sure. I'm supposed to meet him tomorrow – he wants to see my photos. I hoped to get away early, but the meeting is at eleven. What a pain. I don't know why I agreed."

"That's the wrong attitude. When the great man calls you must answer that call! For your country!"

Henry's mock-heroic speech made her smile.

Then his expression changed. He looked troubled.

"Seriously Kate, be careful what you're getting into."

"I suppose you don't like his politics—"

"It's not that. That's different." He paused. "There were rumours about him. Haven't you heard?"

"No. What kind of rumours?"

"About how he got to be the candidate to be an MP. I don't like passing on gossip, but…"

"Go on, spill the beans, you've started now."

"He was assistant to the previous MP, Bill Lurie. Apparently Bill had some kind of illness. It wasn't schizophrenia – something similar. He'd had it for years, was taking medication. It was under control, but he kept it quiet – people didn't know.

"There was a leak, somebody told the media. People said it was Warren, but nothing was proved. He denied it, of course. When it came out there was a big fuss. Then Warren, and others, started saying it was affecting Bill's work. In the end, he resigned. And guess who took over as the next candidate? Your friend Jeremy Warren. Convenient for him."

Kate sat in silence, thinking about Henry's words.

"There's no proof about this, but be on your guard."

"Okay. Anyway, that's enough about me," Kate said, "what've you been up to?"

"I've got a good short list of properties. One went under offer, because we weren't quick enough. But I can't make any decisions without Sandra. It'll all work out for the best in the end. So, you're going home tomorrow Kate, unless the honourable Mr Warren asks you to stay?"

She made a face.

"Seriously, we must keep in touch. I hope you come and visit us when we get settled. You'll like Sandra."

"Of course, I will, I'd love to meet Sandra and you've been a real friend. Thanks for everything."

After she left Henry, Kate thought about Jeremy Warren. If what Henry said was true... But there were always rumours about politicians. Without proof... Besides, she'd already promised to meet him. In truth, she was curious to find out what he wanted.

Kate packed up her belongings on Friday morning. As she took her clothes out of the rickety wardrobe, a pair of trousers dropped off its hanger. She reached down to retrieve them, and felt something standing on the floor at the back. She pulled it out. An electric fire with flex and plug. While she was shivering night after night, it'd been there all along.

Kate saw the pile of books she'd taken out of the library on the table. She put them in a bag with her camera, she must return them before she went. Looking round the miserable room, she shuddered, before closing the door for the last time.

In the library, Hugh smiled when he saw her.

"Are you leaving us?"

JAY LARKIN

"Yes, I've come to return the books." Placing the bag on the table, she piled the books in front of him. Her forehead furrowed. Were there only four? Wasn't there a fifth? She took everything else out of the bag but no more appeared. She must've been mistaken.

"I've got these, but I think I took out another one as well. Can you check?" she asked Hugh.

"Sorry, our system's down at the moment – not an uncommon occurrence, I'm afraid. But don't worry, I'll be in touch if it's missing."

"Thanks for all your help, Hugh."

"Sorry to see you go, hope to see you again." He seemed about to say something else, but hesitated. She checked the time.

"Got to dash. Bye."

On her way out through the lobby, Mr Radcliffe stopped her.

"Thank you so much, Miss Fielding. Your kindly stepping into the breach – the photographic breach – was much appreciated. We are most grateful. Mr Warren was also impressed. When might we see the fruits of your labour?"

"I'll send you the photographs as soon as I can and I'll let you know when the rebranding job is finished."

He kept her talking until she barely had time to gather her belongings together if she was to make the meeting with Jeremy Warren on time.

Kate couldn't find a parking space near the constituency office, so she had to grab her laptop and run from the car. She arrived breathless at the shopfront that bore Jeremy's name in large letters, and found herself in a room full of people. Jeremy Warren's sidekick, Tris, referred to it as the MP's surgery. The people were constituents waiting to speak to him.

"Mr Warren will see you soon, Miss Fielding," he said.

The time of her appointment was meaningless, as several people

86

went in to see Mr Warren before her. After half an hour, she was thoroughly fed up. She owed the MP nothing and was tempted to walk out, when Tris called her name and escorted her into another room.

Jeremy Warren, his stocky figure and blond hair, filled the small space. He stood up and shook her hand with a practised smile.

"Ah, the photographer, delighted you could come."

He might've been welcoming her to a garden party.

"Sapplewood School – such an important local institution – font of learning. Education, vital, vital. The ceremony – great PR for the school."

Not too bad for him either, presumably, that's why he'd held the stage.

"So, er," he clearly hadn't been briefed on her name.

"Kate."

"Yes of course, Kate, I knew your first name, but your surname is?"

"Fielding."

"So, Kate, did you bring your photos, I'm dying to see them."

"I'm afraid I haven't had time to download them yet."

"I see. That's a shame. Have you got your camera with you, could I see..?"

"I'm afraid not."

There was a note of finality in her voice that he couldn't miss. In fact, she could've got the camera from the car, but she was still smarting from the way he'd embarrassed her at the ceremony.

The MP's face cleared.

"You could send them. If they're any good – and I'm sure they will be – we might be able to use them for my publicity material." He beamed at her as if he expected her to be ecstatic at the

JAY LARKIN

honour.

Kate's brow furrowed.

"I took the photos for publicity for the school. Mr Radcliffe..." she paused. What exactly was the position with the headmaster? He hadn't mentioned payment.

"I quite understand," said Jeremy, "but surely, we could come to some agreement... After all, we're on the same side. We all want the same thing."

She disliked his assumption – the implication that she supported him politically.

He leaned confidentially towards her.

"Kate, I'd love to invite you to have lunch with me at the house – the dining room at the House of Commons. You'd find it an interesting experience, a chance to see our leaders up close as well as a great view of the Thames."

She was too surprised to answer.

"Tris will fix up a date."

Just then Tris knocked and opened the door.

"Jeremy, there's rather a traffic jam out here."

"Okay, we're just finishing up. So, Kate, I can count on you for the photos? Tris, please give Kate our contact details and fix a date for lunch at the Commons."

He rose and shook the bemused Kate's hand. Outside, the ever-helpful Tris agreed a date for the lunch and gave her his e-mail address.

"If you'd be good enough to forward the photos to me... so kind."

He turned away. She'd clearly taken up enough of his valuable time.

On the journey home, Kate thought over the meeting. Lunch with an MP at the House of Commons – she was impressed in spite of her objections to Jeremy Warren. But she understood, providing him with the photos was to be her side of the deal. She wouldn't be bullied. She'd choose the photos she needed and send him the rest.

She sighed, more relieved than she'd realised to get away from the school. And tomorrow she'd meet up with Luke.

It wasn't until the next morning, Kate realised something was wrong. Her camera was missing. She searched the car, her suitcase and other bags again and again, not willing to acknowledge the truth. In her haste to get to the meeting on time, she must've left it at the school. This was a blow. The thought of losing her expensive camera... She immediately called the school. The switchboard menu led only to voicemail. She tried to call Adam, but his phone was switched off. There was only one solution, she'd have to return to Sapplewood.

CHAPTER 5

"**I**'m so sorry," Kate said to Luke. She phoned him as soon as she realised the problem. "I've tried ringing, but no one's answering – and I must get the camera back."

"I understand Katie. You absolutely must."

There was silence.

"Maybe we can get together tomorrow, or next week," she said.

"I haven't told you, but I'm going away on Wednesday – not a long trip – but I have stuff to do tomorrow."

"Oh Luke, I don't know what to say."

"Hang on a minute. Let me think. Can you give me a few minutes, before you leave?"

"Yes, I'm not even dressed."

"I'll call you back."

Cursing Mr Radcliffe, Jeremy Warren and Tris, but most of all herself for her carelessness, Kate got ready.

Her phone rang, it was Luke.

"Hey Katie, I've decided. I'm coming with you. We can talk on the journey."

"But it's two hours to the school – and then back. Your day will be ruined."

"It's ruined anyway if I can't see you, so what's the difference?"

"But going to the school, you said…"

"I don't plan on going inside. I'll wait nearby for you. If you don't want me to come…"

"Of course, I want you to come. Thanks so much. I'll pick you up."

That changed things. Luke's company would make a huge difference. They could have a proper chat. It was so sweet of him – especially given his feelings towards the school.

"Where are you off to next?" she asked once they were on their way.

"Tanzania again. There are some problems with the project I set up. I wanted to talk to you about the job, they're offering me a different position. More of a manager. Based here, liaising with different projects. Still travelling, but shorter trips, just to check up on things."

"How do you feel about that? You've always been so hands on. Helping people face to face, on the spot."

"That's true… it's rewarding helping individuals directly. But lately I've been feeling… like it's more about me than them. I'm getting more out of it."

"Surely that's good – altruistic?"

"No – it's difficult to explain. As if I've got this need – to fill some kind of empty hole inside me. And the hole keeps getting bigger. I've wondered if it's guilt – because of everything I've had – all the advantages. And they've got so little. Or maybe it's something else. That's what I've got to decide. I'm forty-two, it's time to take stock, see where I want to go in life."

Although she was driving, Kate turned her head to look at him.

"Is there someone?"

"No – keep your eye on the road – I want to be alive to make the decision."

"For selfish reasons I'd love you to be around more. But do you really want that?"

"There comes a point in everybody's life when they have to think about the future."

"You sound as if you're sixty. What's brought all this on?"

"I've just been thinking. That's partly why I'm coming to... to the school. I've avoided thinking about it for so long. Maybe that was wrong. Unhealthy."

Kate kept her eyes on the road.

"Do you want to talk about it?"

"There's not a lot to say. I don't remember much. I've kind of buried it. If I'd had a chance to talk about it at the time... but there wasn't anyone.

"After I got to your place, I was bundled off back to my folks. You don't really know my parents. They're not like yours. They don't believe in talking about things, problems. Like, if you don't talk about something it'll go away. If you don't say it out loud it doesn't exist. Anyway, now I'm rambling. You don't want to hear all this."

"But I do – it's part of you – who you are. It's true I hardly know your parents. They always seem very – pleasant."

"Oh yes, everything's always pleasant. Nothing's allowed to be... awkward, messy. It was because my father – working for the Foreign Office – he was used to smoothing things over. Hiding or ignoring inconvenient facts.

"I told you I had some sort of breakdown at school, that's why you came to fetch me. When they got me home, they never even mentioned it. Just carried on as if I was back because the school term had ended early or something. They left me alone for a day or so and then said I should make an effort. Behave normally. I still felt bad – depressed, anxious but they wouldn't let me see a doctor let alone a therapist. It was the old cliche, pull yourself together. I realised afterwards, the Foreign Office, especially then, frowned on any type of mental problem. My parents wanted me to go into the Foreign Office like my father, so we had to keep my breakdown secret. Something like that on my records would be a disaster. They never called it a breakdown. Just said I was 'under the weather'."

"It must've been awful. What did you do?"

"I started going for long walks in the countryside. That helped. And horse riding. Then swimming in the summer. I started to feel better. Then my father was posted to the US, Washington. There were plenty of good schools nearby, I didn't need to board. It was a fresh start."

"I'm so sorry, I never realised any of this."

"How could you? You were younger. And I don't talk about it. Really, this is something new. But when you mentioned you were at Sapplewood, it brought back…"

"I'm sorry, if I'd known… I didn't want to upset you."

"No, in a way I'm glad you did. It's upsetting but maybe I need to confront… what happened there. But this is getting heavy, let's talk about something else."

Before they reached the entrance to the school, Kate pulled into the side of the road and stopped. She didn't want Luke to be spooked by the sight of the black iron gates, as she'd been.

"Hope I won't be too long; I'll leave you the keys, " she said.

She went straight to the room where she'd been staying. It hadn't been touched. As musty and depressing as usual. Shivering, she searched everywhere several times, but the camera didn't appear. Had she definitely left it there? Could someone have stolen it? Maybe the school office would be open now. She walked slowly back to the main building, trying to remember when she last saw the camera. The door to the main building was open and a few boys hung around in the lobby, but the door to Mrs Anderson's and Mr Radcliffe's offices was locked. There was a sign giving an emergency contact number as well as that of the school matron. The loss of her camera could hardly be classed as an emergency. Kate stood outside wondering what to do next.

"What do you want?" a brusque voice inquired. It was Ned Hurst, the maintenance manager. The man who'd shouted at Glen in the woods.

"I've lost my camera. I left it in the school, but I don't remember where."

His expression didn't change.

"Come with me," he said and set off across the lobby.

She followed him into a corridor and out the back of the building, but instead of turning towards the place where she'd been staying, he went in the other direction, towards an outbuilding. There was no one else around and it was very quiet. Mr Hurst stopped outside the door and pulled a huge bunch of keys out of his pocket. They were attached to a chain as if he was a jailer. He unlocked the door.

"In here."

The room was dark and smelled musty. Kate felt a prickle of fear run along her spine. What was going on? Surely her camera couldn't be out here. There was no one within earshot. She kept between him and the door, ready to get away if she had to. He marched over to a large metal cupboard and once again, out came the massive collection of keys. He unlocked the cupboard and the metal door squeaked in protest as it opened.

"What are you doing back there? Have a look inside."

Was this a ploy to get her away from the door? Nerves jangling, she cautiously approached the cupboard and peered inside.

"Lost Property," he said.

The cupboard contained shelves filled with all manner of

objects: sports gear, items of clothing, pairs of glasses – and a camera.

Kate picked it up. It was hers.

"Thank you so much. I'd given up hope... so kind of you..." she babbled. She was so relieved to get her camera back, she almost hugged him, her fears forgotten.

His expression softened.

"I was a bit harsh with you the other day. It's Glen – I suppose I'm overprotective."

"I didn't mean anything," she said, "but I saw photos of him for the website. I thought he was a normal... I mean he was just one of the teachers."

Ned's bushy eyebrows knit together.

"That was a right farce. The guy taking the pictures, he said most of the teachers didn't look right. They were too old or too young. Adam with his ponytail – it was the wrong image for the school. He saw Glen, said he was photogenic." he emphasised the last word and snorted. "Huh. They cleaned him up – did his hair, put someone's clothes on him. He didn't understand what was going on, poor fellow. The photographer was thrilled. He took a load of pictures." His scowl was now ferocious. "All a sham. A pack of lies. Dressing him up, treating him like a performing monkey."

"I'm so sorry, what a horrible thing to do. I can't believe they would go that far."

Recognising an ally, Ned relaxed.

"I try and keep him out of mischief. It's not easy. The boys start on him. Pretend to be his friends. They think it's funny to get him to make a fool of himself. He plays along, but he can suddenly turn on them. It's their fault, they just get him worked up. He's got a temper."

He looked as if he could have continued, but snapped his mouth shut.

"I'd better get on. At least you've got your camera back," he said gruffly. He locked the door and stomped back to the main building.

What a relief. And how foolish she'd been. But it was the place, the school. The atmosphere made her nervous.

After Kate dropped Luke off, she returned home and climbed the stairs to her flat. It'd been a good opportunity to talk to him, especially as he was going away again soon. Interesting he was thinking about a management job with less travel, he wouldn't even have considered that up till now. How nice to have him around more.

The next day, she uploaded the photos she'd taken of the ceremony at the school to her laptop. The first ones – taken furthest away from the stage – weren't great. But when Kate reached the later ones, taken after Jeremy Warren had called out to her from the stage, she slowed down and examined each one carefully. There was no denying it, the pictures were excellent, as good as a professional. These were the compositions she'd captured at speed in a room full of people. Maybe she should take a photography course.

The final photograph she'd taken was of Jeremy Warren as he left the hall, turning back at the door to wave at the audience. Kate remembered her relief at that point. She scrolled on automatically, even though she knew it was the last picture she'd taken. How strange. There were other photos on her screen. Had she forgotten about them? She sat up suddenly, staring at the screen with wide open eyes, hardly able to believe what she saw.

She gazed at the images. She definitely hadn't taken them. They were quite different to hers. These were amateurish, taken at night so it was hard to see what was going on. Making out images of trees, Kate realised the final half a dozen photos were all taken in the woods at the school. Examining them more closely, she distinguished the shadowy form of a small building – it must be the shed she'd seen. So charming in the sunlight, darkness gave it a sinister aspect. There was a bonfire near the shed, and this threw light on several figures dressed in dark garments, which obscured their faces and bodies. She studied all the images. The figures appeared in different positions, performing a kind of dance around the fire. In some of the pictures their arms were raised.

She sat back. Who'd taken the pictures? Why had they used her camera? What was going on by the shed in the woods at night? Who were the mysterious figures?

So many questions, but no answers.

After Kate had been back from Sapplewood for a week, she was surprised to receive a phone call from Hugh, the school librarian.

"Hello Kate, I hope I'm not disturbing you."

"No, it's fine. What can I do for you?"

"It's just a small thing – I've only just got round to checking. The book on the school's history you borrowed, it doesn't appear to have been returned."

"Yes, I thought there was one missing. I didn't see it in my luggage. But I'll have a proper look and get back to you."

"Don't worry at all, whenever you have time."

She'd been through her luggage several times looking for her camera, surely, she would've seen the book. But in the end, she found the slim volume in a side compartment of her bag. She rang Hugh back to apologise and promised to post it.

"It was stupid of me to have missed it. I went through my bag about ten times because I lost my camera."

"Oh, that's a shame, it must be expensive, did you get it back?"

"Yes, I'd left it at the school. Somebody handed it in to Lost Property. I could've returned the book then if I'd realised."

"Don't worry, there's no hurry."

There was a pause.

"By the way, Kate, there was something else. I'm coming up to London on a Saturday – the 15th. I wondered if you were free... If you wanted to get together for lunch?"

This request took her by surprise.

"I'll just check. Sorry Hugh, I've got something on that day."

"That's fine. Another time."

Was he asking her on a date? It wasn't clear. She could've cancelled her other arrangement, but he'd caught her off guard, and she couldn't make a decision on the spot.

Kate flicked through the book in case she'd missed anything important, before returning it. There was a short section she hadn't noticed, called 'Ancient History'.

She was right, the school woods were a couple of centuries older than the school itself. They were part of a larger area of woodland, known as Sapple Woods. She read of a legend that an old man had lived in a cottage in the woods with his grandson. Local boys had frightened and threatened him. There were clearly hooligans in those days as well. These activities got out of hand one night, when the boys made a fire too close to the cottage and it burnt down with the old man and his grandson inside.

She shivered. Was the modern day shed on the site of this earlier structure – the scene of such a terrible occurrence? Accompanying the text, was a crude woodcut of the scene. Leaping flames consumed the building and several unidentified figures cavorted around. Kate thought for a moment and then brought up on her screen the mysterious photos that had appeared on her camera. The ones she had no knowledge of. The images were eerily similar to the woodcut. Could there be a connection between the horrific deaths so many years ago and the recent photos?

A few days before her lunch at the House of Commons with Jeremy Warren, Kate selected the photos she needed for the school publicity, and sent the rest to Tris. She received an immediate reply thanking her, probably an automated response.

Having no experience of such an august venue, Kate asked her friends what to wear for the occasion and one of them turned up on her doorstep with a beautiful navy designer suit. When she put on this elegant outfit, she couldn't help getting excited. If only her dining companion was someone else. However, she needn't say much, no doubt he'd talk about himself. She arrived early at Westminster, hardly believing she'd be allowed to enter the iconic building. She showed the guard her invitation, he checked his list and thankfully she was on it. He phoned for someone to fetch her.

The ubiquitous Tris arrived and she followed him to an unremarkable office.

"Please take a seat, Miss Fielding, Mr Warren will be here directly."

He sat down and started working. About ten minutes later, he answered his phone. After a brief exchange, he stood up.

"I'm sorry, but I'm afraid Jeremy's been delayed. He asked me to take you down to the dining room."

So that was the plan. Impress her with the invitation and then fob her off on Tris. Just like a politician. Now he had the photos, she was of no more use and not worth his attention.

Tris passed through the dining room and led Kate onto a broad terrace overlooking the Thames. She couldn't take her eyes off the view. The London Eye was unmistakable and Tris pointed out the other familiar buildings that lined the river. She wished she had her camera.

"Can I take photos?" she asked.

"I'm afraid not." Jeremy Warren himself answered her question. "Thanks for being so patient, Kate. It's alright Tris, I'll take over now."

She'd misjudged him.

"Magnificent, isn't it? No photos, I'm afraid. Sorry to disappoint the photographer."

After drinks on the terrace, they sat in the dining room. The majestic, wood-panelled chamber was redolent of rich food and history, and paintings of former statesmen solemnly regarded the diners.

When they'd ordered, Jeremy leaned towards her.

"Thanks for the photos, Kate, they're superb. So, if you're not a photographer, what are you exactly?"

She explained the situation and he nodded.

"It's not a bad idea to rebrand the old place. Sapplewood has changed quite a bit since my time, and of course the publicity material should reflect that. What other kinds of projects have you done?"

Contrary to her expectations, the man seemed genuinely interested in her. He asked intelligent questions about her work and listened to the answers.

Kate recognised some of the other diners in the room from the news and Jeremy pointed out others.

After they finished eating, Jeremy sat back.

"Kate, I'm always looking for good people to join our team. It's no secret that I'm ambitious and I'm aiming high. The right image for a politician is crucial these days, and I need people to help me achieve that.

"This is the way I like to work with someone new. A potential team member. We give you a small job and if that turns out well, there could be opportunities for future collaborations. What do you say? Interested?" Jeremy's complacent smile indicated the questions were superfluous. He knew it was an offer she couldn't refuse. And he was right. Even a small contract from him would be a huge feather in her cap and could lead to all kinds of possibilities. Whatever her own political affiliations – and these were not strong – working for such a high-profile figure would open many doors. They shook hands in his office and Tris escorted her back to the entrance.

In the end, Kate finished the rebranding project for Sapplewood School a week earlier than the deadline. It was a good piece of work and she was proud of it. She emailed Mr Radcliffe and soon afterwards he called her.

"Thank you, Miss Fielding, for completing our little project so promptly, I am eager to see the results."

She remembered Adam's warning.

"I can let you have part of the work now; I'll attach my invoice and as soon as I receive payment, I'll send the rest."

She did so, and Mr Radcliffe rang her again.

"Thank you for the sample, but I'm afraid I cannot send payment until I see the completed work."

"Mr Radcliffe, I can do that, but the pages will be watermarked. This is normal practice before payment." She applied her standard, transparent, unobtrusive watermarks to all parts of the work. Mr Radcliffe could see everything but couldn't use it in its current form.

Next morning, he was on the phone again.

"Miss Fielding, I do not understand. Every image is obscured by some kind of mark..."

"Yes Mr Radcliffe, I told you the work would be watermarked."

"But I didn't understand, realise... I can't evaluate the effect. Please be so good as to remove them and resend the work."

"I'm afraid I can't do that. I will need to receive at least part of the payment first."

"I am disappointed, Miss Fielding, I thought we had a rapport, a friendly relationship."

She ignored his remarks and he continued.

"I suppose a small sum... as a deposit."

"That might be possible, but I'd require a deposit of fifty per cent of the total figure."

"Be reasonable, Miss Fielding. I cannot possibly hand over fifty per cent of the price without being sure the work is satisfactory. You must understand my position. I am not a private individual; I have to justify every payment to my Board of Governors."

"Mr Radcliffe, even with the watermarks, surely you can judge if you are satisfied with my work?"

"I'm afraid not, as I said it's not me... I cannot authorise payment with the watermarks. I assure you, once I receive the work in its final condition, I will send the money immediately. I am hurt at your lack of trust."

In the end, he wore her down ,and against her better judgement, Kate agreed a deposit of thirty percent. Once she'd received it, she sent the files without watermarks. However, she heard no more from the school. After a couple of days, she rang the head.

"Mr Radcliffe, I haven't received the remaining seventy per cent of the payment."

"Ah yes, yes."

"You promised if I sent you the final version, you'd pay me straightaway. Is there a problem?"

"Well, now you mention it, there is. As I said, Miss Fielding, I could not judge the work with those watermarks covering the pages. It seemed alright, but now I see it without the marks – I'm afraid I'm not satisfied. The work is not what I expected."

"I'm sorry, I don't understand."

"From our original discussion, I was led to believe – to expect – something different, better. Frankly now I see the final version, I don't believe it is worth any more than we have already paid you."

Fuming, Kate put the phone down. Mr Radcliffe couldn't bully her; the terms of their agreement were clearly stated in the contract. He hadn't got a leg to stand on. She'd sue him. But where was the contract? She searched the file again and again. What could've happened? Then she remembered. They'd never actually signed the contract. He'd said something about the printer not working and she hadn't followed it up. Was that a deliberate ploy? It didn't matter. Without a contract she was helpless. He'd outsmarted her.

CHAPTER 6

Kate wondered if she'd hear from Jeremy. Would the politician really offer her work, or was it all talk? But a couple of weeks later, she received an e-mail from Tris, on Jeremy's behalf, saying he'd recommended her for a graphic design job, and asking if she was interested. The brief was attached.

Surprisingly, the project was unconnected with politics. Someone called Anna Clarke wanted to rebrand her natural skin care range. Kate studied her current website. She saw potential, and a good deal of scope for improvement. An interesting assignment. She wondered how Anna was connected to Jeremy. There was no explanation in the e-mail. She replied immediately and Anna got back to her. She sounded excited.

"I'm so glad you're interested. Jeremy gave you a glowing reference. There's a lot to show you and talk about. Up till now I've been working from home, but now I'm renting a shop. It's a chance to develop and become more professional. Would you be able to come here for the day? Where're you based?"

It turned out Anna lived in a hamlet in Jeremy's constituency, only half an hour from Sapplewood School. They agreed a date.

Kate rang Henry, with whom she was in regular contact. He and Sandra had exchanged contracts on a property and he was renting a two-bedroom cottage in the interim.

"I'd love to come and see you – I won't be that far away."

"Why don't you stay over?" he said, "sounds like it'll be a busy day. You can have a meal here and then go home the next day."

"That'd be lovely, we can have a proper chat."

So, on the appointed day, Kate set off early and by ten thirty was driving into the pretty hamlet. Anna opened the door with a wide smile. Her wavy dark hair hung loosely round her face and she wore a floral midi dress. She led the way into a large country kitchen with old fashioned units and exposed rafters. There were enamel jugs of flowers on the long wooden table and children's drawings on the walls. On a crowded pine dresser stood a collection of photographs.

"My kids," said Anna, "Isabelle, Sophie and Hannah – they keep me busy." she grinned.

"Is he yours as well?" Kate pointed at a photo of a boy with jet black hair, a dark complexion and large bewitching black eyes.

"No, that's my nephew. We just make girls." Her tone was no longer merry.

 At the kitchen table Anna showed Kate her current products and packaging.

"I know these are a bit basic, but they really work and they sell well. People say I should charge more and I was thinking if they looked more... classy... better designs, I could raise the prices."

Kate agreed.

"What about the shop?"

Anna showed her photos.

"It's quite small and I can't afford a refit, but I'm going to have it painted. I thought you could help me choose the colours – in line with a new brand."

"Yes and the shop sign..." said Kate her eyes shining. They looked at each other and grinned.

The morning flew by, fuelled by mugs of coffee. Anna had cleared the table and was setting out salads, when the doorbell rang. A man came into the room. He was well built and would've been six foot tall, if he'd stood up straighter. He had the same dark hair as Anna, but his was heavily peppered with grey.

"Kate, this is my brother, Eddie. How're you doing, old boy?" she asked him with a concerned look. He seemed much older than her – more like a father.

He sighed and shrugged. Then held out his hand to Kate.

"Eddie De Vere, pleased to meet you."

He sat down heavily.

Kate stared at him. De Vere was the name of the boy who died at Sapplewood School two years ago. Max De Vere. An unusual name – could Eddie be his father?

"You'll stay for lunch, of course?" Anna asked her brother, her hand on his shoulder. He nodded with an attempt at a smile. As they ate, he relaxed.

"So, what are you two girls up to?"

"Business," said Anna, "Kate's helping me with the rebrand – remember I told you? It's exciting. She's a graphic designer – Jeremy recommended her."

"Good old Jeremy," Eddie said vaguely.

Anna turned to Kate.

"We all grew up together, Jeremy lived near us. Of course, I was the little sister, trailing along behind." She laughed, "I cramped their style when they were home from school."

When they finished eating, Eddie prised himself up from the table.

"I'll be off. Leave you girls to work in peace. A pleasure to meet you, Kate."

He walked out of the room with the shambling gait of an old

man. Anna followed him.

"Take care of yourself, old boy."

She sighed as she sat down.

"I worry about him."

Here was an opportunity to find out about Max De Vere, but Kate must tread carefully.

"I've heard the name De Vere before, at Sapplewood," she said, "an accident… was it?"

Anna nodded.

"It was awful. Just awful. It more or less killed Eddie. You saw the picture." She pointed towards the photo on the dresser. "That's Max. He was special. Even at that age he had – charisma. Though he liked to get his own way. He twisted everyone round his little finger – with one look of those eyes.

"Max was everything to Eddie. Ever since he was born. And then he died. In that terrible, senseless way. That was the worst thing for Eddie, what he couldn't take. He was ill for a long time afterwards, depression. It's hardly surprising he's aged so much."

"I'm so sorry," Kate said, "did they ever find out what happened?"

"There was an investigation – of sorts. The police looked into it, of course. But the school… The headmaster made out Max was unstable, had problems. If Eddie hadn't been in a state of collapse, he'd have forced them to look into it further. But he was too far gone. The school said they'd take measures to stop it happening again. But I don't know."

She got up, opened a drawer and took out another photo.

"This is Eddie with Max and Ratna, his wife. She was a lovely person." She sighed.

"What happened to her?"

Anna contemplated the picture.

"When Max died, it destroyed Eddie. And the marriage. Ratna moved to America and I'm afraid I've lost contact with her." She handed Kate the photograph.

They were an attractive trio. Max got his dark complexion and coal black hair from his mother. Eddie's arms were round his wife and son, and all three were laughing.

There was a silence until at last Anna sat up.

"I'm sorry for going on, I don't want to waste your time."

The two women worked hard and at five, Kate left with a clear vision of what she had to do. Anna was a delightful client, enthusiastic, clear sighted and quick to catch on to new ideas. Kate was excited by the project.

Kate got caught in the rush hour and by the time she drew up outside Henry's tiny cottage, she was weary. The sight of his beaming face cheered her up.

"Wine, Kate? Or something stronger?"

"A shower first, and I must get out of these clothes."

"Ooh," said Henry in his falsetto, "don't mind me!"

They both laughed.

Half an hour later, in her comfortable sweater and jeans, Kate gratefully accepted a glass of wine. They sat in the small reception room that served as kitchen, living and dining room. It was cosy and quaint.

"Sandra will be sorry to miss you, she's up north finishing up things with her old job. So much paperwork," Henry said shaking his head. "Now, what've you been up to?"

Kate told him about her day. When she described Eddie De Vere, he sat up.

"Poor chap," he said, shaking his head. "Shocking business."

He was interested in Anna's description of Max.

"There's something else," she said, "I met this girl Tara..." as she described the conversation Henry frowned. He prepared their meal as she continued to talk.

"So, from what Tara said, Bryan could've got Max to meet him at night, got him drunk and there was an accident. Or he pushed the boy."

Henry was silent as they started eating.

"Sounds to me more likely the opposite," he said at last.

"What do you mean?"

"Sounds like Max was in control. From what you said, he would've laughed at the man."

"But if he threatened to expose Bryan – get him sacked..."

Henry shook his head.

"The whole setup doesn't sound right to me. And another thing, if Max was planning to blackmail Bryan, maybe he was doing the same to someone else. That's a dangerous business. From what you said about the school, it sounds like Bryan wasn't the only one with secrets."

"Max could've been blackmailing another member of staff," she said slowly.

He looked at her sharply.

"Why? I may just be a daft northerner, but don't you think it's more likely that whoever caused Max's accident – or even pushed him – would be a boy, a pupil. Isn't that the obvious answer?"

Kate's eyes widened. He was right. Why had she focused all her attention on the teachers? There'd been something, a reason. But she couldn't remember what it was.

Next day on the drive home, Kate considered the latest information she'd learned about Max De Vere and his family. Anna had echoed Bryan's sentiments about the boy's attraction and charm, although she hinted he could be manipulative. This tallied with what Tara had said.

Seeing Eddie De Vere, altered and aged beyond his years, Kate could appreciate the devastating impact of his son's death. Compared to the earlier happy family photograph, the man was a shell. Though only two years had passed, would he ever recover? Above all, Kate was left with the question, why would a boy like Max be alone on top of a perilous building at night, with alcohol in his blood? This didn't tie in with anything she'd heard so far.

When she got home, she Googled Edward De Vere. Wikipedia helpfully described his background and meteoric financial success story. The De Veres, an upper-class family, were struggling to maintain a white elephant of a historic country house when Edward was born, though they could still afford to send him to Sapplewood. Anna was mentioned, as his only sibling.

The interesting part came later. Having married soon after university, where he met his wife, Edward started a company in one of his parents' outbuildings. Whether by luck or good judgement, this business catered for a newly emerging niche market, and grew exponentially in a short space of time. It then became clear that the young entrepreneur wasn't merely lucky, riding the crest of a fortuitous wave. He showed himself to be shrewd, with a gift for predicting where and how to develop his business. Having made a lot of money in a relatively short amount of time, he steered the company so well over the ensuing years that it went from strength to strength. Edward's personal wealth was large and grew over the years. His wife was named as Ratna and their divorce, if indeed they were divorced, wasn't mentioned.

The final words in the entry made Kate stop in her tracks. When asked the secret of his success, Edward was quoted as saying.

'Everything I've done is for my son. To give him the best life possible and make him proud of me.'

How awful that his beloved son's short life should end in that horrible way. His broken body lying in the dark, on the ground beside the chapel.

The image was vivid. The extra photos taken in the night at the school came into her mind. They also had a nightmarish quality. Thinking of these, she suddenly remembered something. She knew where she'd last seen her camera, and had a good idea of who'd taken the photos. The question was why.

The last time she saw her camera was at Sapplewood library, when she was returning her books to Hugh. She'd taken the camera out of her bag to search for the missing book. She examined the extra pictures again, thinking hard, then picked up her phone.

"Hi Hugh, it's Kate Fielding. That Saturday you were coming up to London, it's this week isn't it? Are you still coming? My other arrangement's fallen through."

"Yes, I'm still coming. I'm so pleased you're available."

She must get more answers from Hugh.

He was waiting outside the cafe when she arrived and smiled at her with a blush.

"So glad you could come."

Hugh told Kate he was in London to see an exhibition at the British Museum. They didn't mention Sapplewood while they were eating. Only when they were having coffee, did she bring up the subject.

"What's going on at the school?"

"Nothing much," he said, his eyes wary, "just the usual."

There was no easy way to start. She took a deep breath.

"I wanted to ask you about my camera."

He turned deep red and looked down. He said nothing. In a neutral tone, she went on.

"I found some extra photos at the end. Photos I didn't take. Was it you?"

Still flushed, he raised his eyes and looked her in the face.

"I'm sorry, I don't know what came over me. It was an unpardonable thing to do."

"I wouldn't say that. It's not that bad. I'm just curious why. And what're the pictures?"

"I hope you don't think I meant to take your camera, steal it?" he said anxiously.

"No, of course not."

"After you'd gone, I found it on the table in the library. I was going to ring you, but I was busy and by the time I got hold of your number, your phone was switched off."

That must've been when she was at Jeremy Warren's constituency office.

"I took the camera to keep it safe and I was going to ring you again. Anyway, that night... but I suppose you've seen... the pictures. I'm a bit of a night owl and I looked out of my window and saw those hooded figures – a group of them walking along. I wasn't going to report them or anything, I just wanted to get some pictures, watch what was going on. I'll explain why in a minute.

"Your camera was on my table, so I just grabbed it and crept out. Honestly, I was so caught up in it, I hardly knew what I was doing. I followed them into the woods, there were six of them.

It was dark, and they had torches. I couldn't see who they were. In the woods, they came to the hut. I kept my distance and watched. There was wood stacked and they made a fire. Then they started dancing round and shouting. No one could hear or see them there.

"I'm afraid I used your camera to capture the images – probably very badly. I could just about work out how to use it. I decided I'd seen enough and went back to bed. The next day, I realised I'd no idea how to download the pictures. I didn't want you to know I'd used the camera, I felt really bad about that. But I wanted you to get the camera back without suspecting me. I put it in Lost Property. I was sure you'd phone the school and get it back. I can't tell you how sorry I am."

"That's alright. No harm done. I did get it back. So why did you want to capture it? Why the interest?"

He smiled a shy yet proud smile. His eyes shining, he reached into his pocket and brought out a paperback book with a highly coloured cover.

"Because of this."

She picked up the book. *Dangerous Destiny* by Hugo Dean. The name rang a bell, she'd seen other books by the same author.

"What does this mean?"

"I'm Hugo Dean. I'm a writer. A writer of cosy mysteries, actually. I brought the book for you. I thought you might be interested."

She turned the book over in her hand. What a surprising man. Hugh – the mild-mannered librarian.

"If you're a successful writer, how come you stay at the school?"

A wry smile flashed across his face.

"It's the last place I expected to end up. I was a pupil, you know, a Sapling."

"No, I didn't," Kate said.

"I didn't have a particularly illustrious career at the school. At that stage, I hadn't any special talents. I was in the same year as Jeremy Warren and Eddie De Vere – the entrepreneur. Even then they were high flyers.

"I liked books so I became a librarian. Later on, I started writing. And people seemed to like my books. When the job came up at Sapplewood, it was supposed to be a stopgap, but I'm still there five years later. It's the perfect setup. During the term I write and research. I don't earn a lot, but I have plenty of free time. And no cooking, cleaning... I often come up to London at weekends to see a show and meet friends. In the school holidays I travel. I go on all kinds of exotic trips to get background for my books. I don't own a property, but my mother has a flat and I sometimes stay with her. It's worked out well so far. I've written eight books and I'm going strong."

Kate was speechless. Hugh was one of the few members of staff who was happy at Sapplewood.

He went on.

"When I saw the procession at night, the hooded figures, I had the idea I could use it in a book. I've been playing around with a murder mystery set at a boarding school. I've even got the title, *An Educated Corpse.*

"Did you get the idea from Max De Vere's death?"

"So you know about that. No, something that happened years before. When I was at Sapplewood another boy died."

Kate remembered the newspaper article about Max's death. It'd mentioned an earlier accident.

"Who was the boy? What exactly happened?"

"His name was Paul, he was a couple of years below me. He was being bullied. He had bad acne – his face was a mess. Everybody made fun of him. I'm sorry to say I did as well. Schoolboys can be a pretty cruel lot. At the time it seemed funny. I never thought about the effect on him. No one did." He dropped his gaze and spoke quietly.

"He ended up jumping off the bell tower."

"There wasn't any doubt it was – suicide?" Kate asked.

Hugh shook his head.

"None at all. Poor guy."

They sat in silence for a while, until Hugh looked up.

"I'm afraid as an author, one can become a bit heartless. One tends to view a tragedy like that as a potential plot angle." He looked at Kate. "Have you come across the 'Silvans' in your research into the school?"

"No – what are they?"

"They're a sort of secret society of boys. A small group. They dress up, go out at night and do the kind of things you saw in the photographs. The name comes from the Roman and pagan god of forests and trees – Silvanus. It's been going on for a long time, maybe since the school started. Handed over to a new group every year.

"I'd heard about them when I was at school. Everyone wanted to be a Silvan. You had to be invited to join. I'd never seen them in action, so when I spotted them that night I had to see what was going on. I want to put them in the book. I got a bit carried away with your camera," he added shamefacedly.

"Everyone knows about the goings on, but Radcliffe turns a blind eye. They don't do any harm, just high jinks."

Kate said nothing, processing this new information. She remembered Henry's words.

"But couldn't they've had something to do with Max's death?"

He shook his head emphatically.

"Absolutely not."

"How can you be so sure?"

"There's no question of any pupils being involved in Max's death."

"Why not?"

"Because there were no other boys in the school that night."

"I don't understand..."

"That day was the end of the term. School finished for the pupils at lunchtime. They all left then and were signed out. There's always a staff meeting the afternoon of the last day of term, and a staff dinner in the evening. Therefore, all the staff were still at the school."

"But you said Max..."

"Wait a minute, I'm coming to that. Max stayed on at the school that night, because his father was coming to meet with Mr Radcliffe the next day. Eddie De Vere's an extremely wealthy man.

"Mr Radcliffe was trying to persuade him to make a large donation to the school. Really substantial. Eddie was coming the next morning to meet the head, along with a few other potential big donors. They were going to discuss the matter. Mr Radcliffe wanted to show them round all parts of the school when it was empty. With no boys getting in the way – except Max of course. A special lunch was going to be laid on. So, I can say with certainty no other pupils were in the school that night."

This was a lot to take in.

Hugh was going to write a book based on the boy, Paul's, death. That did indicate, as he said, a degree of callousness.

For the first time, she considered the implications of the earlier fatality. It seemed incredible that two deaths occurring in an identical manner weren't connected in some way, even if they were twenty-four years apart. However, Hugh was adamant Paul had killed himself, and suicide brought on by bullying was well-known. She'd heard of copycat murders, but copycat suicides?

About a month later Luke was back in the country and they met up, Kate sensed something different about him. She couldn't put her finger on it. An underlying tension, as if there was something on his mind. After they caught up on all the news, the feeling of constraint grew stronger. He spoke less and soon Kate also fell silent. After a long pause he spoke.

"I wanted to talk to you about Sapplewood."

She turned to him in surprise, this wasn't what she was expecting. She'd mentioned as little as possible about the school.

"I've been thinking a lot on this trip. Trying to figure things out. I'm stuck, I can't move on with my life until I put it behind me. What happened all those years ago.

"It's hard, but I'm sure it's the only way. I have to find out what caused my breakdown. I've tried to remember. Some things are coming back."

He sounded strained.

"If there's anything I can do. I want to help... Do you want to talk about it?"

"Thanks Katie. You're the only person I can talk to about this. And since you know the school..."

"Of course. But have another drink first."

She poured him a glass of wine.

He sipped the wine and then inhaled deeply, as if bracing himself to face the difficult task.

"I tried to remember what happened before you fetched me. In the afternoon, when your parents came, I was in the sickroom. A nurse was there or maybe the matron. I was sleepy, confused. Now I think they gave me something to make me sleep.

"I remember that morning before you came, I was in bed in the dormitory. I was crying, I couldn't stop. The other boys crowded round my bed. I just couldn't stop crying. Some teachers came and then I was in the sickroom. It's all confused. I'm sure something happened in the night. Not in the dormitory... Somewhere else..."

He rubbed his eyes.

"Is that all you remember?" she said at last.

He nodded.

Suddenly her mother's words came back.

'He keeps saying the boy died. And it was his fault.'

"Luke, when did this happen?"

"I must've been sixteen. So it must be twenty-six years."

Kate's heart lurched. Paul died twenty-six years ago.

Luke couldn't have any connection with a boy's death. She knew him – it was impossible. And anyway, Paul committed suicide.

CHAPTER 7

Hugh Davenport kept in contact with Kate and she followed his author page on Facebook and Instagram. However, she was surprised to receive an invitation to the launch of his new book, taking place at the famous Groucho Club in London's Soho on a Saturday night. She was intrigued and bought a new dress for the occasion.

Although aware Hugh was a successful author, she had trouble reconciling this new persona with the gentle, quiet librarian. How would he fit in at the Groucho Club – that renowned haunt of glitterati from media and the arts – as the main attraction?

Teetering on her extra high heels, Kate stood at the entrance to the Mary Lou Room at the club. The decor was simpler, brighter and more modern than she expected. Would she know anyone? Would there be any celebrities? Conscious of the unfamiliar shoes, she stepped carefully inside. She spotted Hugh immediately, looking debonair in a tan corduroy suit and blue bow tie. He was posing for photographs holding a copy of his new book.

She picked up a glass of champagne and studied the other guests. The room was half full and several people looked familiar. Minor celebrities. The most well-known person was Diggory Bell, a popular chat show host. He was accompanied by his latest boyfriend. Kate would've liked to take photos, but decided it would be bad form.

"Hi Kate, fancy seeing you here."

It was Adam.

"I'm surprised to be here. Do others from the school come to these events?"

He shrugged.

"I've never been invited before. I'm only here now because of..." Adam looked at the woman standing next to him. She smiled and grasped Kate's hand in a firm handshake.

"Julia Palmer. I'm the publicist for the new TV show." She laid her hand on Adam's arm. "Babysitting the embryo celebrity. We're producing a book to go with the series, and by chance we're with the same publishers as Hugo. The bosses thought this would be good publicity for Adam. Good practise for him as well."

They chatted for a while, as Julia scanned the room.

"There're a couple of people I'd like you to meet, Adam. I'll get them warmed up and come and get you." She set off with a determined expression.

"She scares me," said Adam.

"She seems ruthlessly efficient," Kate said.

She noticed Adam's clothes for the first time. Instead of his usual black, he wore a bright checked shirt, leather waistcoat and denim jeans.

"What are you wearing?"

He winced.

"I'm not too comfortable in this gear. It's Julia's idea of what a potter should look like. I feel more like a country and western singer. All I need's a hat and a guitar."

"By the way, your mugs are still in the studio, you'd better pick them up soon. Have you heard what's happening at the school?"

"No."

"I've given in my notice, so it doesn't bother me. Radcliffe's up to his usual tricks. He never wanted the studio in the first place. He's got a donation off an old boy for a high-tech lab – 3D printers and stuff. He's taking a load of money, doing a bit of work on the studio and sticking up a big gold sign with the guy's name on. He'd sell his grandmother for a big enough donation. Specially now, I heard the school's almost bankrupt. Some company wants to buy it and turn it into a fancy hotel. They'll probably turn the chapel into a spa.

"You'd better get your mugs; they're starting work on the studio when term ends. They'll probably chuck the wheels and all the rest of the pottery stuff out. I asked Henry – you know he's living in the area now – if he wanted a wheel. We won't be doing any more throwing so I told him to come ASAP."

"Wow," Kate said, "so no more pottery at Sapplewood. What a shame."

"You can have a wheel if you want, I didn't think of asking you."

She shook her head.

"I haven't got the room."

"I'm ready for a change," he said, "a fresh start. I've had enough of the school. Now I've got this TV show, I'll be glad to see the back of that place."

A tall woman with white hair and a surprisingly young face, moved to the front of the room and began to speak in a loud, clear voice. The chattering died down.

"Good evening everyone. Glad to see so many old friends and fans of Hugo. I have the honour of being the publisher of his wonderful books. I well remember when his first manuscript arrived on my desk. It didn't take me long to realise I'd found a real talent. A new mystery writer following in the august footsteps of Conan Doyle and Agatha Christie.

"And I was right. Since then, Hugo has delighted us with an enticing new book every year. His settings are unusual, characters engaging and mysteries baffling. The book-buying public have taken his sleuth, Genevieve Lam, to their collective heart, and eagerly await each new book. So, I present to you this year's sparkling offering." She held up a brightly coloured volume.

"*A Fair Wind for Murder*. It's set aboard a luxury yacht, where Genevieve is one of the guests on a private cruise. A real closed circle scenario, where she uses all her deductive powers to solve the murder.

"Hugo actually sailed on a similar cruise for his research – which shows how dedicated he is to his work." Mild laughter rippled round the room. "And on that very cruise, there was actually a man overboard. Apparently a much rarer occurrence than one would think. Luckily, he was rescued or there would've been a real death at sea.

"As usual, Hugo is hard at work on his next book. I can give you a teaser. It'll be set at an exclusive boys' boarding school. I was privileged to get a glimpse of some early chapters about three years ago. As is sometimes the way, Hugo felt the story needed to percolate for a while in his brain before finishing it. But look out for it next year under the title *An Educated Corpse*."

"Anyway, that's enough from me. Eat and drink up everyone and don't forget to grab your copy of *A Fair Wind for Murder*."

Enthusiastic applause followed.

Kate thought about *An Educated Corpse* and remembered the night-time photos Hugh had taken with her camera.

"Adam, do you know anything about the Silvans?"

He turned sharply.

"What did you say?"

She repeated the question.

"No, nothing."

But the hand holding his glass shook, belying the answer.

People were milling around the tables of books, taking copies, and leaving. Others were still arriving and Kate recognised a few faces from the media.

"How do you fancy all this?" she asked Adam, "your new life."

"You mean decent money for a change? I think I can cope. And time to do my own work. I miss it. Making pots. I've got lots of ideas. New things I want to try."

"Sounds exciting."

He gazed over her shoulder into the distance as if picturing future possibilities. Suddenly he inhaled sharply. His eyes widened as if seeing something shocking. He staggered. Kate turned to see what he'd been looking at. Nothing special was going on, just more people arriving. She recognised one of these as Eddie De Vere.

She turned back to Adam. The colour had drained from his face, and he held onto the back of a chair.

"Are you alright?" she asked.

Breathing fast he was unable to speak. The eagle-eyed Julia had noticed and rushed over. She forced an elderly woman out of her chair, sat Adam down and dispatched Kate for water. When she returned, Adam was still pale. Beads of sweat stood out on his forehead. He sipped the water.

"He needs air," said Julia, walking over to a window. "These don't open, I don't know what happens if there's a fire. Let's go outside, Adam."

"I'm all right now," he said, "but I've had enough of this place. I'll get a taxi back to my car."

The colour was returning to his face and his breathing had

slowed down.

"Let me at least get you a taxi, humour me." Julia said with a wry smile.

He stood up.

"Bye, Kate."

"Hope you're okay," she called.

What'd come over him? The room was crowded, but not stuffy or hot. Anyway, he seemed to be in capable hands. Kate took another glass of champagne and surveyed the chattering crowd, her eyes drawn back to Eddie De Vere. She stared at the tall, grey-haired man. This wasn't the shambling, stooped, prematurely aged Eddie she'd met before. Now he stood up straight, radiating confidence and power. There was a good reason for the change. On his arm hung a ravishingly beautiful young woman with undulating waves of glossy black hair. Considerably younger than her escort, she must be a model. Kate didn't expect Eddie to remember her, but he waved and brought over his stunning companion.

"It's Kate isn't it? Eddie De Vere, we met at Anna's place." With a proud smile he looked down at the girl by his side. "Priya darling, this is a friend of my sister."

The girl's smile revealed perfect white teeth. She shook Kate's hand.

"So pleased to meet you."

Kate could hardly take her eyes off Priya's cream silk dress, which shimmered against her dark skin. Seeing the direction of her gaze, Priya laughed.

"It's gorgeous, isn't it? I wasn't sure it'd be suitable – this isn't my usual milieu. By the way, I love your shoes."

Kate grimaced.

"I'm beginning to realise how uncomfortable they are."

"Can I get you ladies drinks?" Eddie asked, "they do the best cocktails in town."

Both of the women nodded.

"What do you do?" Kate asked Priya, with a pretty good idea of the response.

"I'm an accountant," was the surprising reply. "This is all new to me. What about you?"

Responding mechanically, Kate reeled at the information. Beauty and brains. Eddie returned with the drinks. He put his arm round Priya.

"Getting on alright?"

"Eddie, why exactly are we here?" Priya asked, "I know it's a book launch, but..."

Before he could answer, they were hailed by another guest.

"Eddie, Kate – all my friends are here!"

It was Jeremy Warren. Now Hugh himself approached the group.

"So glad you could all come – Eddie, Jeremy, Kate er..."

"This is Priya, Hugh; my fiancée."

"Eddie, we weren't going to say anything yet." Priya's shy smile showed she wasn't sorry about his announcement. Jeremy clapped Eddie on the back and took the opportunity to kiss Priya, which made Eddie frown.

"We must have a photo," Jeremy called over the photographer, "the three of us. My old school friends. Saplings must stick together." He positioned himself between Hugh and Eddie, his arms round their shoulders.

Someone else hailed Eddie and he took Priya away to be introduced. Jeremy moved on – looking for another photo op and Hugh shook his head.

"We were in the same class, but he barely knew I existed. Him and De Vere, they were the 'cool kids'. I wasn't. Now it seems we're best buddies."

"That's what fame will do," Kate said.

In the taxi on her way home, Kate thought about the evening. Hugh, Eddie and Jeremy had all been at Sapplewood together, they were the same age. In spite of the rejuvenating effect of Priya, Eddie still appeared older than the other two.

Kate slept late the following morning and was woken by her phone. It was Henry.

"Sorry to disturb you, but I thought I'd better let you know. Something's happened."

His voice sounded anxious. Now she was wide awake.

"What's the matter? Are you alright?"

"Yes, it's not me. It's Adam."

"Adam – is he okay? What's happened? Where are you?"

"I'm at the school. Adam said they were getting rid of the pottery wheels, and I could have one if I was quick. We arranged to meet this morning, outside the studio at ten.

"I was here first and I went into the studio. It was awful. Somebody's trashed the place. Looks like they took a baseball bat... almost every piece of pottery was smashed to pieces. It feels so... vindictive." Henry's voice shook.

"But what about Adam?"

"He didn't turn up. I tried calling but his phone must've been switched off. There was no one in the office. In the end I found someone who knew where Adam lives. I went there and he was completely out of it. He must've been very drunk, or... I don't know, Kate, maybe he was drugged. I thought you'd want to know. Now I understand how you feel about this place. Something's wrong here."

"But I saw Adam last night. Up in London."

"Did he have a lot to drink?"

"No, I don't think so. He certainly didn't seem drunk. Although he didn't feel well, came over faint. He left early."

She told Henry about the book launch.

"His car's outside," he said, "he must've driven home alright. I'll try and speak to him and get back to you."

Something had happened to Adam at the party. Could he have been drugged? Or when he got home? Someone from the school?

Kate saw Henry had sent photos. She gasped. They were of the pottery studio and it was worse than she imagined. The place was a wreck. No doubt her mugs had been destroyed, but this seemed irrelevant. Who could've done such a thing? What was their purpose? Henry was right, the senseless act was disturbing.

Henry rang later to report on Adam. The potter had a thumping headache, but was otherwise alright.

"By the way, your mugs are okay, almost the only things that are. A chap called Ned – in charge of maintenance here – he's been clearing up with one of his men and I gave them a hand. Although it looks bad, there's no real damage to the building or equipment – it's the boys' work – a real shame. I hope they've taken photos."

"Did you get your wheel?"

"Yes, the wheels are pretty tough. Ned helped me load it in the car."

"Has Adam said what happened last night?"

"He doesn't remember anything. I think he drove back from London and went to the studio for some reason. When he saw the state of it, he went home and drank himself silly. I found some bottles..."

As if that wasn't enough excitement, Kate received another unexpected phone call later that day.

"Hello, Kate, Eddie De Vere here. Good to see you last night. Hope you enjoyed the party."

"Oh, yes. Hello – er – Eddie."

"I'm ringing to sound you out about a new project I'm starting. I'm looking for good people, and Jeremy Warren – and Anna of course – have been singing your praises."

"Thanks," was all Kate could mutter.

"This new idea – well it's something exciting. Close to my heart. To tell you the truth I haven't been this interested in anything for years."

"What sort of project?"

"Bear with me, Kate, I'm not going into details yet. There's going to be a meeting where I'll be presenting the idea to a select few – potential team members. I'll explain everything then. Sorry to be so mysterious, but all will be revealed.

"I wanted to ring you myself, but my assistant will be in touch with the details. I hope I can count on you to come along. No obligation of course. Just hear me out. Anyway, great to catch up. See you soon."

He hung up.

What was that all about? The only thing that was clear was Eddie had taken it for granted she'd fall in with his plans and attend his mysterious meeting – whenever it was. She didn't get a chance to say a word in reply. Obviously, he was used to getting his own way. However, it was flattering to be invited.

Almost immediately, an e-mail arrived from Eddie's assistant with details of the time and place of the meeting. It was to be a few days later, on a weekday evening, at an office in central London. A light supper was promised. Kate checked her diary and clicked the accept box. How could she resist such an invitation?

Kate entered the plush meeting room in the smart office. Eddie was already there and so was Priya. The latter wore a well-cut navy suit and white silk blouse. Her glossy hair was pulled back and she wore dark rimmed glasses, but still looked stunning. She gave Kate a shy but warm smile. Kate sat down and helped herself to water. The room filled up and soon twelve people were seated around the table. Eddie stood up and they waited expectantly. Before he could begin, the door opened and Anna rushed in.

"Sorry, everyone..." she called.

Eddie waited for her to sit down and then began.

"Welcome one and all. Delighted you could come. I'm sorry to be so mysterious, but now all will be revealed. As I told you, I'm embarking on an exciting new project. Dedicated to him."

On the screen behind Eddie appeared a large image of his son Max. The boy's looks were striking.

"I believe you all know, this is Max. My son, who..." Eddie gulped, pressed his lips together and continued with a noticeable effort. "Max passed away in a terrible accident two years ago." Once again he collected himself. Priya and Anna looked at him anxiously.

"I speak as a proud father, but it was generally agreed, Max was a special boy. Charming, clever, with great ability. A beloved boy." Eddie picked up his glass and drank. "As I say, Max was talented in so many ways. But his most unique strength and first love –

was music. He was a gifted performer, playing piano and guitar. But more unusual for someone of his age, he was a composer. A composer with huge potential. He could've been..." He paused to take a deep breath.

"At first, after the accident, I could do nothing. But now I feel compelled to honour Max. Some good must come out of this appalling tragedy." Eddie paused and his audience waited. Priya put her hand over his and Kate noticed Anna frown.

"After a great deal of thought, I've decided the best way to honour my son and create something good in his name. I'm going to establish an organisation to help young composers – others like Max – to achieve their potential. I'm lucky enough to have the funds to conduct this project in the way I wish.

"The details are not yet decided, but I plan to buy a property which can be converted into a centre where young composers will receive training, help, guidance and the opportunity to have their work performed. I want to bring top musical experts from around the world to teach and support these young people.

"The idea is to select a cohort of the most promising young composers, from all walks of life. The centre will provide residential accommodation for students and teachers."

As Eddie spoke, his eyes lit up and his tone grew excited and enthusiastic as he described his vision. "The young people will attend their normal schools, and the programme of events at the centre will be held at weekends and school holidays.

"One detail I know for sure is the name. I've thought about it and decided on 'Max's Composers Of Tomorrow – M.A.S.C.O.T."

Eddie was breathing fast, and as he finished, his audience clapped loudly. It was impossible not to be moved by the man's depth of feeling. He smiled, "Thank you all," and continued.

"First, we need the right team to make this dream of mine come true. I expect to employ one or two full time project managers and a number of freelance specialists as and when needed.

"This is where you come in," he said nodding around the table. "you've all been invited because you have the skills we need. I want to emphasise, that although we will be operating as a charity, everyone will be properly compensated for their work." He paused, "I'm sure there's a lot you want to know, so now I'll take questions, feel free to ask anything."

Few people asked questions and an awkward silence ensued.

"Supper will be served and while we're eating, please come over – I'll be glad to explain anything." Eddie said, "If you'd like to get involved with this exciting enterprise – and I urge you to do so, please sign up. There are several sheets around the room."

The information in Eddie's speech was a lot to take in and Kate hesitated before signing up. The door opened and waiters filled the table with a generous selection of finger foods. Anna came over and hugged her.

"Good to see you," she said, "Eddie told me you were coming. What do you think?"

"It's an interesting idea…"

"Yes, I'm so glad Eddie's ready to get back into the fray. He looks much better, don't you think?"

Kate nodded.

"Definitely."

"Are you going to sign up?" Anna asked.

"I'm not sure, I don't want to commit… I know it's a good cause, but…"

"There's no obligation, Eddie just wants to get an idea of who might be interested. By the way, I'd really like to catch up with you," She glanced round the room, "away from… everyone. I'm staying over tonight, at Eddie's place, and it's not far. Do you fancy a drink?"

It wasn't late and Kate was intrigued.

◆ ◆ ◆

"It's just round the corner," Anna said, as they left the building, and led the way around a square. "There's a gorgeous garden, lovely in the summer," she said, "quiet and private – only for residents." Kate peered through the iron railings to see shadowy trees, and paths winding around the grass.

Anna stopped outside an imposing building, with a marble lobby and concierge, who greeted her. Coming out of the lift into a thickly carpeted corridor, she unlocked the door and they entered the flat. Although the block was an older one, Eddie's flat was decorated in fashionable shades of grey. The rooms led off a small entrance hall and Kate followed Anna into a large open plan area. There was a kitchen – surprisingly small – but Eddie probably never cooked. The capacious seating area contained a charcoal grey L-shaped sofa, matching armchairs and other top-quality furniture and accessories. The style was masculine – if Priya was living there she hadn't yet made her mark on the furnishings. On the walls, Kate recognised artwork by well-known contemporary artists.

"That's a Damien Hirst isn't it?"

Anna nodded, smiling at Kate's shocked tone.

"Yes, I'll show you round." Anna kicked off her shoes and wriggled her toes. "I don't know how people can walk around in heels all the time."

"Vanity greater than comfort."

Next to the living room, was a formal dining room, with a table that seated ten.

"They never use this," Anna told Kate and showed her the three en-suite bedrooms – all the furniture and fittings were of the highest quality and taste.

"Now the surprise," she said, going over to the small kitchen area. She opened a full-length cupboard door to reveal the entrance to another room. A decent-sized, well-equipped kitchen.

"This is where the real cooking happens, the other bit's just for show and drinks." She shut the secret door and collected glasses and wine.

"I've never seen anything like it. Such a clever idea," Kate said.

"What did you think about this evening?" Anna asked.

"It sounds like a good idea."

"Yes, it's great to see Eddie getting excited about a new project. Don't you think he looks better? Younger?"

Kate nodded.

"Definitely."

Anna's forehead wrinkled.

"What do you think of her?"

"Who?"

"Priya."

Kate hesitated.

"Young and – pretty."

"Yes, and a gold digger." She spat out the words.

Afraid of saying the wrong thing, Kate said nothing.

"He's known her about two minutes and suddenly she's his fiancée. It's quite obvious what she's after. I'm surprised he can't see it. It'll end badly."

Privately, Kate thought Priya was responsible for Eddie's improved looks and interest in the project, rather than the other way round.

Anna sighed.

"She's staying here with him, you know. I just hope he doesn't rush into anything. But he's besotted. Won't listen to me. Are you going to get involved in the project?"

"I think so. It sounds interesting. Are you?"

"No, I was only there for moral support. I've got my business and the kids. To be honest, I don't even like coming up to town anymore. Now that she's here."

They sipped their wine and then Kate asked,

"Was Max really as angelic as Eddie said? Obviously, a dad is biased, and of course I know he was your nephew..."

Anna answered after a pause.

"He loved Max very much – was so proud of him. Other people saw things in the boy – but Eddie would never hear a word against him. There was something," She looked into the distance, "years ago. Max came over to play with my girls, he was about ten. My girls are younger. While he was there, Hannah had an accident. Fell off a high wall and broke her arm. We didn't see it, but the girls said it was Max, he'd made them walk along the wall. They'd never done that before. All three of them were adamant it was him.

"I had to say something to Eddie when he came to pick Max up." She thought for a while. "I don't know what happened. He took him in another room. When he came back, Eddie was full of excuses, said Max wasn't used to girls, it was just high spirits, but I could see he was troubled. Max was pale, it was the only time I saw him like that. He was rattled. So, Eddie's aware of what Max could be like." She shrugged, "Or at least he was then.

"It would've been better if they'd had more children. They both focused on Max too much. I believe in a bit of healthy neglect. They tried – went to specialists, had treatment..." She shrugged. "There are some things money can't buy."

While she was talking, there was a noise in the hall. The sound of the front door opening and laughing voices. Eddie and Priya came in. He had a huge grin and Priya was glowing. He waved a bottle of champagne.

"Hi Anna, Kate. Glad you're here. You can help us celebrate. We've set the date for the wedding."

"Congratulations," said Kate and Anna muttered something unintelligible. Eddie and Priya didn't notice her lack of enthusiasm.

"No need to tell everyone straightaway, why not keep it in the family for the moment?" Anna said.

Eddie and Priya looked at each other and burst out laughing.

"I'm afraid that's going to be difficult," he said, "the restaurant where we were eating – where it all happened – the press were there, photographers..." he grinned, "it'll be all over the newspapers tomorrow." He hugged Priya. "Anyway, I want everyone to know how happy we are. It's no secret."

"He's not as important as he thinks," Anna said in the hall as she said goodbye to Kate.

However, she was wrong. Eddie was a well-known figure, Priya was attractive and love stories are always popular. There were photos of the happy pair in the newspapers, but that wasn't all. Kate received a cryptic message from the newly formed MASCOT WhatsApp group,

BBC, tonight 8:30, Diggory Bell Show.

She turned on the TV at the appointed time to show the opening titles of the popular chat show. After Diggory's welcome, the screen cut to a photo of Eddie and Priya drinking champagne. And there they were, sitting on the sofa opposite him, holding hands and smiling. The fawning Diggory treated them like minor royalty, asking questions about their romance in reverent tones. Eddie answered confidently, Priya interjecting smiling comments.

When the story of the romance had been fully explored, Eddie brought up the topic of MASCOT. Diggory had clearly been primed for this and allowed him to talk fully and fluently about the project. Eddie looked at the camera.

"I am, of course, the first patron of MASCOT, but I hope others will join me in supporting this exciting cause."

A photo of Max was shown on the screen and as the host wished the happy pair rapturous congratulations, the MASCOT website was displayed at the bottom of the screen.

Kate sat back. What incredible publicity. Was this all planned? No matter, the programme would give Eddie's project a tremendous boost. Kate no longer had any doubts. The chance to get in on something like this. On the ground floor...

CHAPTER 8

After Eddie and Priya's appearance on TV, things went mad. As soon as the programme finished, Kate checked the URL that'd been shown on screen and found a basic website – a temporary placeholder to give the public somewhere to register interest. A short while later, she got a WhatsApp informing her of an urgent meeting the next evening at Eddie's office.

The atmosphere at the meeting was quite different from the last one, the excitement in the room palpable. The same people were there as before, apart from Anna, but also several new faces. Kate noticed a middle-aged woman with lavender-coloured hair, equally colourful clothes and masses of wooden jewellery. The noise died down when Eddie started speaking.

"I certainly didn't expect our next meeting to be quite so soon, but things have moved on." He smiled at Priya.

There was clapping, cheers and shouts of congratulations.

"We must strike while the iron's hot and use the publicity to our best advantage. We need to move quickly. I take it you're all committed to the project?"

Once again the response was loud.

"Now we're forming our team, I'd like to introduce everyone." Eddie pointed at Priya. "Priya Basu, project manager. We're looking for a full-time admin assistant for her.

The door opened and all eyes looked at the newcomer. It was Jeremy Warren. He walked slowly towards Eddie, his smiling glance moving round the room, gathering attention. He raised his hand.

"Hi everyone. I heard your call to arms on TV," he said to Eddie in a voice that was meant to be heard by all, "and here I am. Your next patron." He smiled at the applause.

Kate watched Eddie. A frown crossed his face, but he quickly recovered.

"Mr Jeremy Warren, MP," he said, "Good to have you on board." They shook hands and Jeremy stood by the table while a chair was quickly found for him. He sat down next to Priya.

Eddie continued round the table, announcing names and job titles. There were individuals with skills ranging from IT, finance, architecture, to PR and social media management. He paused at the woman whose colourful hair and clothes had caught Kate's attention.

"Posy Pittou," he began.

"Wordsmith," she interjected.

"Yes, Posy writes books for children," Eddie tried to move on to the next person, but Posy took no notice.

"I have a special affinity with the young," she clasped her hands together, her bracelets clanking, and looked earnestly round the room. "Max – the darling boy – I knew he was a unique soul."

Everyone's a unique soul, Kate thought, not warming to Posy.

"I felt called upon to help. To keep his spirit alive." Posy closed her eyes and subsided back into her seat.

"Finally, last but not least," Eddie indicated a thin, intense looking man. "We are delighted to welcome on board Martyn Gesso. Martyn was involved with the National Youth Orchestra for many years. We can learn a lot from that organisation. It has similar aims – giving young musicians opportunities for learning. Martyn has agreed to act as our consultant."

Some people around the table applauded.

The rest of the meeting was spent thrashing out goals and plans for the organisation and allocating tasks. Kate was to devote as much time to MASCOT's permanent website and branding as possible. Fortunately, her other work wasn't demanding at that time.

A couple of days later, checking social media, Kate stopped scrolling in disbelief. Posy Pittou, aka the woman with the lavender hair from the MASCOT meeting, had written a blog post on her website that'd gone viral. It was entitled, 'Max De Vere and Me'. In the post she reiterated her close relationship with the boy. They were 'kindred spirits' and she indicated she was the only one to really understand him, appreciate his true nature. After everything Kate had found out about Max's character, she was shocked at Posy's description of a 'pure soul', 'noble nature', 'prince among boys'. According to her, Max was only one degree lower than the angels. Without furnishing details, she mentioned acts of kindness, compassion and empathy beyond his years.

The whole piece made Kate feel queasy. She wondered what Eddie would make of it. It was one thing not to speak ill of the dead, honour a father's grief, but this... The MASCOT project was a worthy one, but if Posy's words or similar featured in the MASCOT literature, knowing what she did, how could Kate accept it? She sighed and wondered what to do next. She didn't have long to wait. WhatsApp messages were pinging on her phone. There was one from Eddie to the MASCOT team.

Neither I nor MASCOT endorse Ms Pittou's remarks. She is no longer connected with our organisation or authorised to speak on our behalf. Don't respond to her post or anything else she writes.

It was a shame to start the new project in such a manner. What could Posy's motive be? Self-aggrandisement or something else?

Kate couldn't avoid seeing the correspondence around the offending post and soon found the answer to her question, when the author announced the launch of her latest children's book. She declared it was inspired by and dedicated to, 'a special boy'. The cynical conclusion was that Posy hoped the publicity Eddie and MASCOT had generated, would encourage the sales of her book. Kate returned to work on the MASCOT website, relieved that Eddie had seen through Posy.

The following day, Kate received a call from an unknown number. The unfamiliar voice asked,

"Miss Fielding? Geoff Dawkins here. English master at Sapplewood."

"Hello Mr Dawkins, what can I do for you?"

"I wonder if I might speak to you – in person. Am I correct in thinking you're involved with Mr De Vere's organisation – in memory of his son, Max?"

"Yes, but…"

"Would it be possible to meet sometime over the weekend? I believe you're based in London. I can come up by train. It's important."

She agreed to meet him at a cafe.

Mr Dawkins had given no clue of what he wanted to talk about.

The schoolteacher was already seated at a table in the corner of the café when she arrived.

He stood up.

"This is good of you, Miss Fielding."

"Please call me Kate."

"I'm Geoff."

They shook hands. When cups of coffee were in front of them, he seemed reluctant to start. He sipped his drink, staring down at it and then took a deep breath.

"You were probably surprised when I mentioned – what's it called – MASCOT?"

Kate nodded.

"Mr De Vere has certainly attracted a considerable amount of publicity," he said, "it's a good cause – giving support to musical youngsters." He paused. "The fact is – some of the publicity – the information that's been on the Internet..." he leaned towards her and lowered his voice.

"Do you remember, Miss, er, Kate, that I told you about a boy I encountered, who had—" He looked over his shoulder, but no one else was in earshot, "psychopathic tendencies. Who was... sadistic. That was actually Max." He watched Kate closely, his body tense.

She sat back in her chair.

"Oh, I see."

He went on, speaking in an urgent tone.

"I'm sorry for any father that loses his son. A boy who dies in such circumstances – it's natural to focus on the positive. But quite frankly I can't stomach some of the things that've been written about him."

Finally, Kate had an inkling of what he was trying to say.

"Do you mean Posy Pittou – her blog post?"

He nodded unhappily.

"I know you're working with her – she's part of the organisation, but it's not right, the way she describes his character. She's making him out to be a saint."

Kate listened in silence.

"If the organisation is going to use such language in its literature, to gain support, I believe it's wrong."

Geoff sat back and exhaled, as if he'd said his piece. He raised his coffee cup and drained it.

Kate thought before replying.

"I've heard disturbing information about how he spoke and behaved from other sources, too. As you say, obviously Eddie – Mr De Vere – may not see it. May not want to see it. Especially now. And it's not right for MASCOT to present a false picture of Max.

"But Geoff, you don't need to worry. I felt the same as you. I was uncomfortable with Posy's stuff on the Internet. But Eddie had no idea she was writing those things. She's no longer in the organisation – I don't think he wanted her to start with – and we've been told to have nothing to do with her."

Hearing Kate's words, he sighed.

"That's a relief. Ready for another cup?"

When he'd brought the coffees, Geoff returned to the subject.

"What made her write about Max like that? Did she know him well?"

"I don't think so. She lives in the block of flats where Eddie has his London base. From what he said, Posy bumped into Max a couple of times when he was there in the holidays. She can't have exchanged more than a few words with him."

"Then why...?"

"She's a writer and she's got a book coming out. Her own reasons for wanting publicity."

He shook his head in disbelief.

"Since we've got things clear about Max, what he was really like, I want to tell you about my personal experience with him, is that okay?"

She was intrigued.

"Yes, if you don't mind talking about it."

"I'd like you to know. It illustrates his character. The story starts quite a while ago, more than ten years. I came to Sapplewood then because of friends of mine, Mike and Jill. He'd been my best friend since university, and when he married Jill, we all got on well together. Unfortunately, when he was only forty-five Mike was diagnosed with multiple sclerosis. He had it badly.

"They lived near the school; they'd moved into a specially adapted bungalow. I wanted to be close, so I could help out. There happened to be a vacancy at Sapplewood and I got the job.

"As Mike got worse, I spent as much time as I could with them," he stopped speaking and looked down at his hands. Kate waited. With an obvious effort he continued.

"Things turned out…" he sighed, "No, that's not true, we knew what we were doing. Jill and I, we… Mike never knew," he said quickly, "we were very careful, discreet. We kept our relationship quiet for years."

Kate wondered what this had to do with Max De Vere.

He went on.

"Then out of the blue it happened. Max was one of my pupils. A reasonably good student: his grades were satisfactory. Music was his strength, that's where he put in the effort.

"He asked to speak to me, I didn't know why. He came to my office and sat down." Geoff frowned. "There was something about his expression, an air of superiority. He lounged back in his chair. Then he came out with it. He'd found out about Mike – and my relationship with Jill – I have no idea how. He said it was his duty to tell Mike. He sat there with a smirk on his face waiting for me to take it in.

"At first I thought he'd ask me to give him better grades, extra help, but he just sat there. As if he owned the room. Smiling and slouching in the chair. He asked me what I thought, shouldn't he tell Mike the truth?

"Then I realised – he wanted me to collapse, beg him not to tell. Acknowledge his power over me. This was fun for him, to control me. No doubt he would've hinted at the secret whenever he wanted to torment me." Geoff sat up straight.

"I've never been so furious in my life. Not for myself, not even for Jill, but for Mike. We knew then Mike didn't have long left to live. The idea that after keeping it quiet for so long, that little bastard was going to destroy Mike's last few months." He almost ground his teeth at the memory. "But somehow, I found the right words."

"I looked Max straight in the eyes – he wasn't expecting that. I told him I wasn't afraid of him, but the slightest whisper of this'd better not get back to Mike – or anyone else. I was angry, but I didn't shout, my voice was calm. I spoke slowly, deliberately. If a word of this got out, I'd go straight to his father.

"I'd heard he was close to his father, but I didn't know if the threat would work. Max's expression changed. He went pale and sat up straight. I said I'd tell his father what he'd done. Did he want his father to know what kind of vicious, sadistic bully he had for a son?

"I saw the horror in his eyes. I knew I'd hit on the right weapon, his one area of weakness. He looked down. Beaten. He slunk away."

"Still, harrowing for you, I guess," Kate said, her eyes narrowing.

"I got over it," he shrugged, "Max kept quiet and Mike passed away a year ago. In peace."

Kate looked at her watch. Geoff noticed.

"I'm sorry, I've taken up too much of your time."

"It's fine. I was just thinking, do you fancy lunch? There's a pub round the corner that does a great ploughman's."

"If you've got time. There was something else. About Max."

They decamped to the pub.

"You said there was something else?" she prompted, when they'd finished eating.

"Yes," Geoff replied slowly, "it concerns a colleague at the school, so I won't tell you all the details."

"It must've been six months or so before Max... died. A member of staff was having trouble with their computer. The school machines are not the latest and this particular person wasn't very comfortable with technology. Max saw their struggles and offered to help. It occurred to me later that he might've tampered with the computer and caused the problem himself. Anyway, he helped, apparently out of the goodness of his heart. After that, there were other issues with the machine and Max was always ready to help.

"The member of staff began to rely on him, and lose confidence in their own ability. Panic if Max wasn't around. Then he – Max – dropped the bombshell. He said the computer system in the school was antiquated and his father was going to replace it completely. He talked about Macs and how different it would be. This terrified my colleague. It was generally known Max had a lot of influence over his father's decisions. He persuaded Mr De Vere to cough up – for something for the music department. And he got his father to change his mind about giving money for some sports equipment.

"My colleague knew Max had the power. The boy also mentioned he'd be too busy to help out in the future. He expressed serious concerns as to how they would manage the new system without his help. The member of staff was frightened. They relied on the computer to do their job."

Kate regarded Geoff closely, trying to recall something. He looked at her in surprise. She remembered a conversation she'd overheard in the staff room.

"Mrs Anderson," she said, "are you talking about Mrs Anderson?"

Geoff looked round to check no one was listening.

"As a matter of fact, I am. You seem remarkably well-informed. Since you already know, I suppose I can confirm her identity. The whole thing was very unpleasant. It may not sound much, but Pat was seriously distressed." He thought for a few moments.

"I wouldn't be surprised if he'd made up the whole issue just to torment her. Mr De Vere may've had no intention of such an action."

"So cruel," Kate said, shaking her head.

For a while she pondered what she knew about Max.

"I've heard of others," she said looking into the distance, "he – I suppose tormented is the right word."

"Yes, after what he did to me, I kept my eye on Master Max. The strange thing is I didn't see any evidence of him bullying other boys – pupils. That sort of behaviour would seem more likely. He targeted staff members, adults."

She turned to Geoff.

"Do you know about the Silvans?"

"So, you've heard about them as well? I can't believe you were only in school for a week. Yes, of course. It's a long-standing tradition at the school. A bunch of boys dress up in robes, drink a bit and dance around a bonfire at night. It's harmless enough."

She looked at him in surprise.

"But couldn't it be dangerous? You know, initiation ceremonies that get out of hand?"

"No, I've never heard of anything like that. You've got to understand, boys at a boarding school have a more constrained life, away from their families. They need to let off steam, do something that's forbidden. The head knows about it."

Geoff looked at his watch.

"It's later than I thought, I'd better get going." He stood up. "Thanks so much, Kate. Sorry I've got to dash." He held out his hand and she shook it. And then he was gone.

Geoff Dawkins' revelations about Max confirmed Kate's previous assessment of the boy's character. The more she found out, the more potential murderers she discovered. She'd ended up as a sleuth in spite of herself.

Henry rang Kate.

"I've got your mugs from Adam. Do you live anywhere near Rickmansworth? Adam recommended a pottery supplies place there. I'm coming to have a look. Might even get a small kiln."

"It's not too far, it wouldn't take me long to drive there."

"Adam says there's a good pub nearby."

They arranged to meet for lunch the following week.

Kate was already sitting in the pub when Henry arrived. He put a cardboard box carefully on the table.

"Thanks," she said, "have you been to the shop? Are you really getting a kiln?"

They discussed pottery while they ate.

"You also felt the atmosphere in the school?" she said, as they sipped coffee.

"Yes. And you know me, I'm a down to earth northerner. But I was glad to get out of the place I can tell you." His face cleared. "But what's all this I hear about you hobnobbing with the rich and famous? Fancy book launch parties? This new project of Edward De Vere's – very high profile. I'm surprised you still bother with simple folk like me."

Kate grinned.

"Shocking isn't it. But seriously, the project – helping young composers – is a good one. I believe in it."

"They've been painting a different picture of the boy though, than what we'd heard."

"Yes, I know, but that's finished." She told him what she'd told Geoff Dawkins. "We're focusing on Max's musical abilities rather than his character."

"I found out more about Max. And it's not great."

Giving no names or information that could identify Geoff Dawkins or Mrs Anderson, she told Henry what the teacher had said.

He sucked air in through his teeth noisily.

"Sounds like a charming character. Like we said before." His brow furrowed. "And it's adults again he's been bullying, staff."

"Oh yes, I forgot to say. I found out there were definitely no other boys in the school the night Max died."

She explained what Hugh had told her.

"So, if he did meet someone..." he said slowly, "it would have to be a member of staff."

"Yes. And there are a few on the list."

"If we're running with this – and I'm not saying I approve – what about the headmaster, what did you say his name was?" Henry said.

"Really? Mr Radcliffe? What would he have against Max?"

"You said he would do anything for money. If Max knew that – and he probably did – he might play Radcliffe a bit. Threaten to use his influence. About his dad making a donation. You said there was a meeting the day after he died, with Radcliffe and big donors. Maybe Max threatened to put his dad off, and that could affect the others. Of course, all this is just guessing."

"I suppose it's possible. So, the head could also have a motive." She counted off on her fingers. "Mr Radcliffe, Bryan." Suddenly she remembered the gun. She'd assumed Bryan had been contemplating suicide. If Max had been shot... But he hadn't. She went on.

"If we're pushing this – there's someone at the school – a sort of handyman. I heard that the boys take the mick – get him riled up. And he can be violent. Mind you," she paused. "I can't imagine Max meeting him in the chapel at night."

"And what about the girl, Max's girlfriend?" Henry said.

"That's true. She lives nearby, she would've been around. So many enemies," she sighed, "and those're only the ones we know about."

They sat in silence for a while. Finally, Kate stood up.

"I'd better be going. It's good to see you. Let me know if you get a kiln."

She was starting the engine of her car, when Henry came running out, waving his arms.

"Kate," he gasped, breathing hard, "the mugs. You've forgotten them."

Shamefacedly, she went back into the pub.

"Thanks. I am an idiot. That was the whole point of today." She picked up the cardboard box.

He patted her on the shoulder.

"Never mind. It's always good to see you. I'm just glad you've still got time for a simple old man like me. You haven't had your head turned by your new friends."

Most of Kate's time was now spent working on the MASCOT project. Eddie was keen to get things moving as fast as possible to make the most of its current high profile. There were frequent meetings at his office with the whole team. They were held in the early evening and Kate was often invited back to his flat afterwards. Over pizza and wine, she got to know him and Priya.

The only fly in the ointment was Jeremy Warren. He never wanted to miss out on anything and turned up unannounced at the flat whenever his political activities allowed. He would walk in, sit down and help himself to pizza. As a patron of MASCOT, he was of some help to the organisation and he was an old friend, but Kate sensed Eddie's unease on these occasions.

Kate heard from Anna. Her new shop was doing well and the rebranding was a great success.

"I'm coming up to London for a meeting," she said, "the business is set to expand. Could we get together in the evening? I'll be staying at Eddie's place, but let's go out."

They met at a quiet restaurant, where they could talk. Anna described her meeting with the London store that was considering stocking her products.

"Exciting," Kate said, "that's a big step."

"Yes, another league. I put it down to your designs, Kate, I'd never have got the chance without you."

They talked more about Anna's business and then went on to MASCOT.

"I'm so pleased for Eddie," Anna said, "it's the best thing that could've happened."

"It's taking off so fast," Kate said, "I can hardly believe it."

"I hear you're getting pally with Eddie and Priya."

Kate looked at her.

"How do you feel about her now?"

Anna shrugged.

"I'm fine. I've got used to her."

"I'm pleased about that, I like her."

Anna poured out the last of the wine and sat back. Kate thought for a while before speaking.

"Can I ask you something?"

Anna looked puzzled.

"What about?"

"It's Jeremy. He's always turning up at the flat. He walks in as if he owns the place. I don't think Eddie is too keen. Is he married? What's the story"

Anna took a sip of wine.

"We all go back a long way. He and Eddie were friends at school. They were very different, Eddie was always big for his age, popular – a leader, I suppose. He was good at sports, team captain, that kind of thing. Mind you, he got into his fair share of trouble. The school would be on the phone to my father and there'd be a big row. Nothing serious," she added hastily.

"I remember once there was a fuss about a secret society. Drinking and fooling around in the woods at night. Eddie could talk his way out of anything, even in those days," she said with a rueful smile.

"Jeremy was short, not really sporty. Better at academic subjects. But they always hung around together. He used to come to our place in the holidays."

She picked up her glass and drank slowly.

"Then girls came into the picture. Everyone liked Eddie. All the girls were after him.

"Eddie and Jeremy went to the same university, that's where Eddie met Ratna." She frowned. "Actually, I think Jeremy met her first. They went out for a while, but once Eddie came along, Jeremy was out of the picture. Jeremy has his faults, but that had happened a few times, it can't have been easy for him.

"Eddie liked Ratna, but her getting pregnant so quickly... they hardly knew each other. He was pushed into getting married so young – parents, you know. But when Max was born, Eddie fell in love with him. They both did. Max was what kept that marriage together.

"Jeremy got involved in politics at university. He was ambitious. Out of Eddie's shadow, he did well. He told me his plans once, he wanted to make a career in politics, become an MP. He was really confident then.

"Getting married was part of his plan, but the right marriage. He was quite open about it. He wanted money. Serious money would help his career. Also, he wanted a wife who would fit in, be good at entertaining." She grimaced. "He got the money. Married Charlotte – her family are loaded – multimillions. Her father is Stanley Grey."

Kate's eyes widened.

"Wow. I didn't realise."

"Yes. He's done very well in politics. And her mum's Nancy Santos."

Kate nodded again.

"Isn't she a lawyer?"

"Yes, she's very bright. And she's so charming... witty... Jeremy was dazzled by the money. And her parents. Charlotte was dazzled by him. She's very quiet, people say she's standoffish, but she's just shy. She's not bad looking but sort of colourless. After they got married Jeremy found out Charlotte wasn't interested in politics. She hates socialising. She likes gardening, baking, homemaking. They've got a house in his constituency in the country, and she mostly stays there with the kids. They've got two girls, they're both just like Charlotte.

"Jeremy is always moaning to me about them. Now he's got

the money he takes it for granted, complains about Charlotte. Says she's a hindrance to his career. He calls the girls 'the white rabbits', and not in a nice way.

"Jeremy's always latched on to anything Eddie does, if there's something in it for him. This MASCOT thing is in the news and being a patron makes him look good. I don't know why Eddie lets him barge in on things."

"That's what I thought," Kate said, "you can tell he doesn't want him there."

Anna's brow wrinkled.

"It wasn't always like that. He was more in awe of Eddie when they were young. Looked up to him. I don't know when it changed," she said slowly.

"How did Jeremy get on with Max?" Kate asked.

"He liked him a lot. Especially as Max got older. Jeremy was disappointed with his own kids. He must've been jealous of Eddie – another thing he could do better. There's been a long list over the years."

"But I suppose Jeremy didn't have much to do with Max." Kate said.

"I'm not sure," Anna said slowly, "I seem to remember him going to visit Max at school. Taking him out for lunch. There was a bit of trouble because you're supposed to get the parents' permission. We went over with the girls once and forgot to speak to Eddie beforehand, we had to get him on the phone before they'd let Max come out with us."

Anna's description of Jeremy's history with her family and current situation explained some things that'd puzzled Kate. But not all of them. Even Anna didn't understand the hold he had over Eddie.

One evening, Eddie arrived at the office brimming over with excitement.

"Great news everyone! We've got an opportunity – an outstanding opportunity. I've been following up every avenue to keep MASCOT in the public eye." He couldn't stop grinning.

"We've been approached by a TV company, they want to follow our progress, film us as MASCOT gets off the ground. It'll be a series, showing viewers behind the scenes. Of course, we'll all have to face the cameras – I'm told you get used to it quickly." He beamed at his team. There were excited and apprehensive looks.

"I'll be meeting with their people ASAP to pitch the idea. We know they're interested, but they have other projects in the pipeline. I want to spend this meeting working on our pitch."

"Will we all have to be on camera?" someone asked.

"You won't have to," Eddie said, frowning , "but I hope everyone will want to. It's for the good of the project."

From his face, Kate guessed that anyone refusing wouldn't have a future with his organisation. A new challenge, it might even be fun.

Eddie and Priya met with the TV company and reported back jubilantly to the team.

"It's in the bag!" he said, holding up a champagne bottle, "we're celebrating. They weren't a pushover – it was touch and go at one stage. But in the end... They're axing another series they were just about to shoot. It's such wonderful publicity for us." He opened bottles and Priya handed out champagne in plastic cups.

Kate had a sick feeling in her stomach.

"What series are they cancelling?"

He looked at her in surprise, and then at Priya.

"Do you remember?"

"It was about pottery, I think," she said.

"Can they do that? Cancel a series after the contract's been signed? A friend of mine was involved in that series."

"Yes, it's standard practice, apparently," Eddie said, "written into the contract. They film a pilot episode and test audience reactions. There's a get out clause so they can cancel at that point. Did your friend get a lawyer to look over the contract first?"

"I don't know, he never said," Kate said miserably.

She grasped her plastic cup, unable to drink. It must be Adam's show. The series he was pinning all his hopes on. The school studio was being converted, and he'd already given in his notice. There'd be no more pottery at Sapplewood.

CHAPTER 9

While he was away, Kate kept Luke up to date with her activities and he was suitably impressed.

"De Vere," he said, the first time she mentioned Eddie, "I remember him. He was a couple of years ahead of me at school. One of the cool kids."

Luke particularly liked the idea of helping disadvantaged youngsters. He told her about a young musician he'd heard of in Tanzania.

"There's this boy – I heard about him from a friend of mine out here. Another colleague was working on a project in a village. He had his guitar with him and he heard a boy, a teenager, singing. The kid, called Ajani, had an awesome voice. They got together and taught each other songs. The guy was there for a while and started teaching the boy to play the guitar. He left his guitar with him when he came back."

"That's interesting, nice thing to do," Kate said.

"That's not the end of it. When he got back home, the guy got in touch with people – charities and others – and told them all about Ajani. Showed them pictures, played recordings. He wouldn't let it go. It took more than a year, but he raised money to bring Ajani over to England and now he's studying. He's got a scholarship at a music school."

Kate repeated the story to Eddie.

"We must speak to the boy, and the guy who brought him over. It's a great story and we might get useful information from them. Where did you hear about this?"

She told him about Luke.

"You should bring him over to dinner when he gets back."

"He's not big on dinner parties, but thanks all the same."

"Alright, we'll eat pizza off the coffee table, could he cope with that?"

Kate laughed.

"I think so."

She wondered about bringing Luke into this new world she'd entered. Luke dealt with the basic issues of life and death in the developing world. He hated the rise of the vapid culture of celebrity. She regarded the MASCOT project as worthwhile and Eddie and Priya as genuinely caring. Would Luke see past their luxurious lifestyle?

After the next MASCOT meeting, Priya took Kate aside.

"There's something I want to ask you." She glanced over at Eddie, but he was talking earnestly to another member of the team.

"The TV company want to film some shots at Sapplewood – for the pilot episode. Eddie's freaking out about dealing with the headteacher. I've said I'll sort it, but I don't know the man or anything about the school." She hesitated.

"You know him, do you think there'll be any problem getting the school's permission?"

"I shouldn't think so, if we're willing to pay. Radcliffe will do anything for money."

"I'm sure we can take care of that. But somebody really needs to visit the school. The TV company want us to provide photos of key locations, like dormitories, the music room..." She grimaced, "and unfortunately also the tower – where Max fell..."

"That's ghoulish," Kate said.

"It'll make good television apparently. Anyway, you can see why I don't want Eddie involved."

"Yes, of course."

Priya paused and Kate realised she had no choice.

"I'll contact the school and arrange to go along. I'll look at the locations and take the photos."

"Thanks so much. That's a relief. I'll send you all the details."

Mr Radcliffe agreed to cooperate, for a price, and arranged for Kate to meet Ned Hurst.

Driving through the black iron gates once again, a familiar feeling of dread tightened her stomach, but in a milder form than before. She drove up to the main building and parked. Early for her meeting with Ned Hurst, she sat in the car to avoid bumping into the head.

The maintenance manager was prompt, took Kate to his office and gave her a surprisingly good cup of coffee. He looked puzzled.

"Mr Radcliffe told me you were coming, but what is it you want exactly?"

She explained the TV company's requirements.

"I suppose so," he said doubtfully, "will they want to film when the boys are here or when the school's empty?"

"I'm not quite sure. We're just at an early stage."

She left the chapel till last and brought it up hesitantly.

"Are they going to film there?" Ned asked incredulously.

"It seems so. They say it'll make good television."

He raised his eyebrows.

"Do you want to go there now?"

"If that's okay."

As they walked round to the chapel, steel grey clouds were massing in the sky, heralding rain and creating an atmosphere of foreboding.

The chapel door was of heavy oak. Ned pulled out his huge bunch of keys, fitted a large one into the lock, and they went in. They both paused inside the doorway. The chapel was long and narrow with pews along the sides. Sombre light filtered in through arched stained-glass windows set high in the walls. Kate detected the faint fungal smell of rotting wood. She seemed to hear the ghostly echoes of sermons delivered by faceless clerics across the years, to hosts of unresponsive boys. This was no place of spiritual solace or inspiration.

For a brief moment, the sun emerged and flooded light into the building, throwing jewelled shapes on the flagstone floor. The flash of light vanished and the interior returned to its former gloom.

Ned marched to the back of the chamber. He pulled aside a curtain to expose a small door which he unlocked. Kate saw a staircase.

"I'll go first. Mind your step," he said.

They mounted the narrow stone stairs in silence. Light reached them from above and they passed two small windows, before arriving at the bell itself. It was smaller than Kate expected, and there was space around it for several people. Curved openings in the square tower allowed the bell to be heard, and revealed an ominous, dingy sky. At night, the stairs and tower would've been in complete darkness. Anyone ascending would need to bring their own light. Had a torch been found in the tower after Max's death, with his body or in the vicinity?

"There's a ledge outside, all the way round," Ned said.

Kate peered through an opening and saw it. A brave – or foolhardy – boy could climb onto the narrow projection and walk around the tower. In daylight, it wasn't that hard, but at night, with judgement affected by alcohol it would be easy to fall. She also saw how a desperate boy could throw himself off the ledge. Alternatively, if a boy was on the ledge, someone inside by the bell could lean through the opening and push him off. It wouldn't require much effort. An easy murder. Kate shuddered.

Then the rain came. The wind drove it into the openings, cascading through from all sides. Kate's thin blouse was soon soaked.

"Let's go," said Hurst.

Teeth chattering, she followed him down the staircase.

Once more back in the chapel, rain slashed against the windows, their colours dim.

"Let's wait a few minutes till it passes," he said and she nodded, shivering. Without a word he took off his tweed jacket and wrapped it round her shoulders.

"Thanks," she said in surprise.

They waited without speaking, the only sound the rattling of rain on the windows.

She remembered something.

"How's Glen doing?"

"He's alright. He's doing what he's supposed to do. He's a good worker if he's left alone."

The sound of the rain, the unnerving atmosphere of their surroundings and Ned's jacket round Kate's shoulders had broken down barriers, creating a kind of intimacy.

He spoke in a casual tone.

"He's my cousin. He was working in a garage, but it didn't suit him. He likes to be around trees, get out in the fresh air, so I got him the job. That was about three years ago."

Encouraged by his words, Kate asked,

"You said boys tormented him – was one of them Max De Vere?"

He stared at her and she wondered if she'd gone too far.

"Yes. He was the worst. Some of the boys tease Glen, but that Max – he went out of his way to find him. And he knew what to do, how to get under his skin." His large hands clenched into fists. "It was like he enjoyed it. Bastard." The last word was spoken under his breath.

"Glen still talks about him; he calls him the devil. I've told him a hundred times that Max fell off the tower, but he says he flew away in the sky. Says a bat came at night to get him." He shrugged. "It's a mystery the way his mind works.

"When it happened, the police questioned Glen. I told them he wasn't up to it. They wouldn't listen. Wouldn't let me be with him. Grilled him for ages." He scowled, "He's an easy target. I could've told them he can't stand heights – you'd never get him up the tower."

"Did they accuse him?"

"At one point. But there wasn't any evidence. They had to let him go." He frowned. "He was in a right state. That's when he started going on about bats and flying."

Kate shivered again and drew the jacket round her.

"I know you're working for Max's dad," Ned said, "but..." He clamped his lips together.

The rain grew harder, hammering on the windows.

"I heard another boy fell from the tower, a long time ago," Kate said.

"Yes. I'd only been here about a year. Awful it was. I was young.

Not used to... life."

"Did you know the boy?"

"No, I was just a gardener then." He paused, "I remember what happened. They found his body in the morning. It was a terrible shock. To everyone. The police came. They took away the... body.

"His family... his mum was crying, couldn't stop. His dad – he walked with a stick; his face was kind of grey. Looked really sick. And there was a kid, younger brother. He was crying too."

He sighed.

"I was so sorry for them. Everyone was."

"How did Paul die?"

"The same way as Max. He fell."

"Was anyone with him?"

"No. They said he was by himself."

"Why would he come up here alone?"

He stared into the distance as if summoning up distant memories.

"I'm not sure. I think he was depressed. Boarding school doesn't suit everyone. There's always the odd boy who can't cope. Homesick. Or they get bullied."

She had to tread warily.

"Did they think he... did it on purpose?"

"That's what I heard. There were other stories going round. But nobody really knew."

He sighed deeply. Clearly Paul's death had affected him more than Max's, even though it was so long ago.

They stood together without speaking, until she asked.

"Do you know anything about the Silvans?"

He scowled.

"Bunch of idiots. Dressing up and prancing around at night. Cause me a lot of trouble. Starting fires. None of the headmasters take it seriously. Part of the school's history they call it. Harmless." He snorted, "nearly burned down the woods more than once over the years, not to mention the shed."

"How often do the Silvans meet at night?" she asked.

"Only a couple of times a year. Lucky it's not more. You never know when they'll start their nonsense. After Max... Mr Radcliffe wanted one of my men to stay up nights to keep an eye on things. The chapel and the woods. You can't expect a man to work day and night, not just for a few quid extra."

The sound of the rain had died down, Ned opened the door and they saw it was only spitting.

"Shall we make a run for it?" he said.

Back in his office, she handed him the jacket.

"Thanks very much for this and your time."

"That's alright. Let me know if you've got any more questions. For the TV company."

On the drive home through persistent rain, Kate thought about her experience in the chapel. Actually, standing in the bell tower made the two deaths more real. And Ned Hurst. Today she'd seen a different side of the man. A sensitivity. He clearly felt protective of his cousin.

Ned was a prosaic, unimaginative man. He took Glen's words at face value and dismissed them as nonsense, but maybe Glen was trying to describe something he saw. When Max fell from the tower it could've looked like he was flying. Was Glen there that night – not inside the tower – but outside, watching? And the reference to a bat, what did that mean? Not a literal bat – but something or someone... An image came into her mind. Mr

Radcliffe, his black gown, with its wide sleeves, billowing behind him as he mounted the stage.

There was something else. Someone... Another memory flitted across her mind. She screwed up her eyes to capture the image... But it was gone.

Kate returned to Paul's death. Ned had been deeply affected by it. Hugh was definite Paul's death was suicide, but Ned's words implied doubt. Had she been too ready to accept Hugh's statement?

All she knew about Paul was that he had bad skin and was bullied because of it. He might've been a random victim. If someone at Sapplewood was a psychopath... Psychopaths kill again, sometimes many years later. They choose similar victims and methods of carrying out their crimes. Was it possible the same person who'd killed Paul had also killed Max twenty-four years later? Was he or she still at Sapplewood?

Kate's heart lurched. Was it somebody she knew?

CHAPTER 10

"Hi, Anna," Kate said answering her phone, "are you coming up to town?"

"Not at the moment." There was a pause. "Kate, I wanted to ask you – how do you think Eddie's doing?" She sounded worried.

"Eddie?" said Kate slowly, focusing her thoughts. "Okay, I guess. In which way?"

"He was down here at the weekend, him and Priya, but... he didn't look so well. Have you noticed him drinking more than usual? I know you see a lot of him, he's always talking about you. Priya as well."

She thought about the last time she'd seen Eddie. It was at his flat. They'd had Chinese.

"Now you mention it, he has been drinking a bit more. Opening extra bottles... Only wine, though, nothing stronger."

"Hmm. That's what happened before. After Max died. I thought it was under control now. Frankly, I'm worried about him."

Kate let her talk without interrupting.

"I was talking to this friend of mine. She was telling me about grief, what happens if someone close to you dies.

"She said there're five stages you have to go through before you can move on. Denial, anger, bargaining, depression and acceptance. You can go through them more than once – in any order. After Max died, Eddie just seemed to shut down, like he was numb. She said that's denial. He was certainly depressed for a long time, but I don't ever remember him getting angry. She said bargaining is like blaming yourself or someone else. Going over what could've been different. He hasn't done that either. My friend said two years isn't that long when you've lost a child. I don't know what to do. I'm down here and he's mostly in London."

"What you're saying makes sense," Kate said, "but he seems okay to me, apart from the extra wine. I haven't seen him angry. But we're not that close." She hesitated. "Have you spoken to Priya about this?"

"No," Anna said in a tight voice, "I can get on with her in small doses, but I couldn't talk to her about this."

"What do you want me to do?"

"I don't really know. Just keep an eye on him. And let me know if he gets worse," she said with a sob in her voice.

"I will. I'll do anything I can."

Anna was right. Even with a new fiancée and the MASCOT project, Eddie was still grieving for his son. Maybe working on MASCOT, focusing so much on Max, had stirred up his feelings, brought them to the surface again. But Eddie was a grown man and her boss. There was little she could do apart from let Anna know how he was doing. If only Anna got on better with Priya.

Kate watched Eddie fetch a third bottle of wine, one evening after her conversation with Anna.

"None for me," Priya said quickly.

"Me neither," Kate added.

Eddie paid no attention, opening the bottle and filling his glass.

Kate picked up the dirty plates.

"I'll put these in the dishwasher."

She was at the flat so often, she knew her way around the kitchen and liked to help.

"Anyone for coffee?"

"Thanks, Kate," Priya smiled briefly.

Eddie said nothing. He sat slumped on the sofa, grasping his drink. He looked little better than when Kate had first met him.

She opened the hidden door into the secret kitchen, stacked the dishwasher and began to clear the work surfaces. Hearing Eddie speak, she stopped.

"My poor boy. My poor Max."

Kate was surprised she could hear him in that inner room, he wasn't talking loudly. The door wasn't thick or closefitting. However, sounds from the secret kitchen – clattering of plates or glasses – didn't reach the sitting room. A strange acoustic effect.

"I never wanted him to go to that school. He could've gone to Eton – anywhere. She wanted him near home. It was her fault. Why did I give in? I should've stood my ground. It was all my fault. With what I knew about the place... And I still let him go there. They said it was cursed... they were right!

"If only I knew what happened to him, why didn't the police find out? They didn't do anything. I can't understand it. Why didn't I insist, push them?"

"Don't blame yourself, darling, it's not your fault," even Priya's quiet words were audible.

"Someone's to blame – whatever happened. The school didn't do anything – Max shouldn't have been in the chapel at night. How could the school let him – that Radcliffe..." His tone was now belligerent.

"All he cared about was money. He was all over me when he

wanted a donation, but when my boy, my poor boy needed help...
Where was he then?"

"Darling, please don't upset yourself."

"My son is dead and nobody cares. I want to know how and why."
Now Eddie was shouting.

Kate felt awkward, a reluctant eavesdropper. She made two cups
of coffee and brought them into the other room.

"I've got to go now, thanks," she said, grabbing her bag from the
sofa.

"I'll see you out, "said Priya, standing up. When they were in the
hall, she shut the door and spoke in a low voice.

"I'm sorry, he's had a difficult day. Some news... we heard that
Ratna – you know – Max's mum."

Kate nodded.

"When Max died, she went to America. She got married. We just
heard she's expecting a baby. It's really upset Eddie."

"That's understandable."

"It doesn't really make any difference to him..." Priya sounded
uncertain. She bit her lip. "Thanks, Kate, you're a good friend."

Thankfully Eddie behaved normally at the MASCOT meetings,
but the next time they asked her back to the flat, Kate agreed
with some trepidation. She needn't have worried. Eddie had
shed his bad mood and was back to his usual self. While they
were waiting for the food to be delivered, he brought up the
subject of Max's death quite calmly.

"I'm not satisfied with the police investigation. At the time, I was
in shock, now I want answers. I'm going to Scotland Yard. I have
influence and I'm going to use it."

He ate heartily and drank only a couple of glasses of wine.

Even when Jeremy turned up, his mood didn't deteriorate. Doing something about Max's death suited Eddie's active nature. Feeling helpless had affected him badly.

Luke had been away for six weeks and Kate was longing to see him. The Saturday meeting was at his place – a small, one bedroomed flat in an unfashionable suburb. He opened the door and greeted her with a hug, the embrace lasting longer than usual.

The flat was sparsely furnished, Luke was used to living in small spaces and his personal possessions were minimal. However, his home was welcoming, with a few well-chosen pictures and textiles picked up on his travels. A bunch of lilies on the table in an unfamiliar vase was a surprise. She'd never known Luke to appreciate flowers before. Lunch was also special, homemade butternut squash soup, lasagne and lemon meringue pie.

"You didn't make all this yourself?" she asked.

"Everything but the pie, but I know it's your favourite."

They talked first of Kate's work and she filled him in on everything she'd been doing.

"So, you're now chums with the famous Edward De Vere? Did I tell you he was a couple of years above me at school?"

"Him and his fiancée are really nice. They've asked me to bring you over to them for a bite one evening. They want to hear about Ajani."

He grimaced.

"I'm not really good at the whole dinner party thing."

"I know, I told them, but could you cope with eating a pizza on your lap on their sofa?"

He smiled.

"If you want me to come."

After coffee, he stood up.

"Now for the next part of the plan."

"Where're we going?"

"How about Kenwood?"

Kenwood House in Hampstead was Kate's favourite place in London. They took the tube to Hampstead, and walked up the hill in the bright sunshine to Whitestone Pond.

"Do you remember when we paddled here?" she said.

"Yes, most of my memories of England are tied up with you," he said quietly.

She glanced at him. He was in a strange mood. They walked across the Heath, enjoying the unspoilt landscape and soft smells of trees and warm grass. Meandering towards Kenwood House, they stopped at a Henry Moore sculpture.

"Do you remember how we used to climb on it?" Kate said, stroking the bronze curves, "it seemed so big."

"I liked the trees better," he said, "there are some great ones to climb here. Do you remember you found that big tree with the hollow trunk? "

When they arrived at the graceful white mansion, sitting on a hill, she sighed with satisfaction. They walked round to the front, and she noticed for the first time that the entrance was of the same classical style as Sapplewood School. A series of pale, fluted pillars, topped by twin spiral scrolls supported a triangular pediment. But here her memories were all good ones.

"Do you want to go inside?" Luke asked.

She looked at him. He'd never been interested in architecture or stately homes.

"What I'd really like is a cup of tea."

"Easily done," he said, and they made their way to the cafe located in the old stables.

But he was wrong. On such a sunny Saturday afternoon the place was packed, with long queues at the counters and every table taken.

"Let's try outside," he said, but the outdoor seating area was equally full.

Their luck was in, however, as they scanned the tables, a couple stood up and Kate darted over to claim the table.

Luke grinned.

"Good work, Katie. Now stay here and guard it with your life, while I get the tea. Don't expect me back anytime soon."

She leaned back in the chair and basked in the sunshine. Scents from shrubs and flowers wafted gently through the warm air.

"Hey, wake up sleepyhead."

He placed a tray on the table. As well as pots of tea there were chocolate brownies.

"You do know it's not my birthday till next month?"

He laughed and poured out the tea. The setting was idyllic, the brownies were delicious and there was enough tea for several cups each.

"This is just perfect," she said.

"That's what I was aiming for. I wanted to talk to you. I've been doing a lot of thinking. Firstly, this business about Sapplewood. I don't want to look into that anymore. I'm ready to move on. I want to let go of the past and look to the future. Let sleeping dogs lie.

"I told you about the job. I've decided to take it. Like I said, it'll mean less trips away and shorter ones. Also, the pay's better. You know I've never been bothered too much about money."

He stopped, his expression becoming more serious. "The flat's been alright up to now. But..."

Suddenly he stood up and grabbed her hand.

"Let's walk."

Puzzled, she let him lead her out. They crossed the sloping lawns away from the house and stopped at the edge of the lake.

"Look at the bridge," Kate said, and they both regarded the graceful white curves perfectly reflected in the still water.

"I remember how upset you were when you found out it wasn't real, that it was a sham, like fake scenery on the stage. You cried. I hated it when you were sad," Luke said softly.

He took both her hands and looked into her eyes.

"Katie, I love you. I've loved you ever since I can remember. It's like you've always been a part of me." His expression changed. "I've never felt worthy of you – I'm still not – but do you, could you…?"

She looked at his anxious eyes in the sunburnt face. His hands grasped hers tightly.

"Luke, I…" Her heart was hammering and she took a deep breath, but still couldn't speak. He looked so worried; she must answer. "It's always been you. No one else."

His face lit up and he pulled her towards him. He kissed her properly for the first time.

They wandered for ages around the grounds, not knowing where they were going. Not caring, just happy to have found each other at last.

They sat very close on the bus back to the station and on the train. Holding hands, they walked to Luke's flat at a fast pace.

Shutting the door behind them, he asked,

"Do you want a drink? Something to eat?"

"No, I just want…"

She didn't finish the sentence as he drew her towards him.

When Kate awoke the next morning, she remembered where she was as soon as she opened her eyes. She turned her head to gaze at Luke, his tanned face dark against the white pillow. As he awoke, a troubled look passed over his face, but changed to a smile so swiftly, she thought she'd imagined it. They ate poached eggs on toast, speaking little, until he asked,

"What have you got on today, Katie?"

"I was supposed to see Angie…" she said, uncertain if he expected her to cancel the arrangement.

"I've got stuff to do as well," he said clearing away the plates.

She sat in silence, wondering how things stood after yesterday's declarations, and the night. They'd been friends for so long, had such an easy relationship. Now it felt awkward. She was unsure and her body grew tense. What was the next step?

"Can we meet up tomorrow evening?" he said.

Weak with relief, she smiled.

"I'll cook."

He hugged her and she turned her face towards him. The kiss was long and satisfying. Everything was alright.

Over the ensuing days, they settled down into a routine. Eating together in the evenings and staying over in one or other of the flats. During the day they resumed their normal activities. Kate moved as if in a dream – a fantasy she'd never dared to imagine. Finally, they were together.

However, their situation also had the unreality of a dream. They should've been at their closest. The magical beginning of a relationship, when everything was fresh and exciting, but without the awkwardness of getting to know a new person. Her happiness should've been complete. And yet… there were times when Luke turned away from her, biting his lip as if struggling to control a troubling emotion. As he slept, he sighed and made short cries of unutterable sadness. She never commented, but wished she could help.

CHAPTER 11

K ate cried off a couple of times when Eddie asked her back to the flat.

"What's up?" he asked.

"Luke's back and..."

"Oh, the wanderer returns. When're we going to meet him? I'm serious, we must make a date."

There was no getting out of it so although he groaned, Luke agreed to Thursday night. He met Kate outside the office after her meeting. They walked round the garden square to Eddie's building.

Luke stopped and gazed at the outside.

"Wow, Katie, I didn't expect this. The guy must be seriously loaded. Are you sure he's not after you?" he said with a wry smile, "I can't compete with this."

"He's got a fiancée who's far more beautiful than me."

"I don't believe that."

"Wait and see. And wait till you see inside the flat."

Luke showed an almost childlike wonder at the elegant lobby and the smart concierge who greeted Kate. He spoke in hushed tones.

"I can't believe this place."

"I suppose I'm used to it."

Kate rang the doorbell and a grinning Eddie welcomed them.

"Eddie, meet Luke," Kate said.

They shook hands.

"Eddie De Vere, pleased to meet you Luke. We've heard a lot about you."

"All good I hope."

Priya joined them and Eddie completed the introductions.

"Come and have a drink."

They went into the living room and Eddie poured drinks. He asked Luke about his work, showing genuine interest. Kate saw Luke stare round the room, fascinated by his surroundings.

"Can we give Luke the tour?" she asked.

"Of course," Priya said standing up.

Luke's eyes widened at the sumptuous bedrooms and bathrooms, but he said little.

"Now for the kitchen," Priya said when they were back in the main room.

He looked puzzled.

"Isn't this it?" he said pointing at the row of cupboards, sink and island unit.

Priya shook her head. She released the catch on one of the cupboard doors, and it swung open to reveal the inner room.

"Eddie likes the open plan living room, but this way you don't have to keep the kitchen tidy all the time."

Luke was enthralled.

"This is super cool! A secret room. Katie, we'll have to get one of these."

Kate heard his words and her heart skipped a beat. Did he

mean…? It sounded like he expected them to get a place together. He'd mentioned his flat was too small for the future. Now her heart was beating faster. Her face grew hot. She checked herself. She was reading too much into a couple of innocent remarks. It was so early in this new phase of their relationship. Luke meant that if he was spending more time in England, he'd need more space for himself. As to the kitchen, he was speaking without thought, excited as a child with a new toy.

They sat down on the sofa and Eddie asked Luke about the Tanzanian boy, Ajani. The two were soon deep in conversation. Priya moved closer to Kate. She inclined her head slightly towards Luke and gave a discreet thumbs up. Kate found herself blushing like a schoolgirl.

"I'm so pleased for you," her friend whispered.

The doorbell rang.

"That'll be the food," said Eddie, "I hear you like pizza, Luke. We weren't sure which topping, so we ordered a few."

Priya jumped up.

"I'll get the door." But returned, unsmiling and empty handed. Someone followed her into the room.

"Evening all," said Jeremy Warren with a general wave. "Reception at the French Embassy was cancelled. The ambassador threw a hissy fit. So here I am. Who's this?" he said looking at Luke.

Reluctantly Kate introduced him and a feeling of constraint came over the room. Jeremy talked to Luke, but soon managed to turn the conversation towards himself.

"I was the first one to spot Kate – it was at that do at Sapplewood – wasn't it, Kate? She took some great photos of me – knew she was good. We're using them in my campaign publicity. And a designer as well. A real talent, our Kate."

Inwardly cringing, Kate forced a polite smile.

"Remember that lunch at the House, Kate? The House of Commons," he explained to Luke, and addressed the room as a whole. "How's Anna?"

Thank goodness he'd finished with her, Kate thought. But her relief was premature.

"I got you that job, didn't I, Kate? You've got a lot to thank me for."

At this point, Priya stepped in.

"How's Charlotte, Jeremy, and the girls?"

He shrugged.

"Alright, I suppose. Don't get down there much. Too busy with affairs of state."

"We must persuade you to get involved with MASCOT. With your experience of the non-profit sector, you'd be a great help," Eddie said to Luke, but Jeremy interrupted and hijacked the conversation. Eddie moved away to an armchair on the other side of the room.

"The food should be here soon, I'll get the plates," Priya said, "and I've made a salad. Come and help me, Kate."

Once they were inside the secret kitchen, Priya turned to Kate.

"Luke's great. How long have you known him? Is it serious?"

She blushed.

"We've known each other for years – we more or less grew up together. But this new relationship – we're taking it slowly."

The doorbell rang.

"I'll get it," Priya said, "will you bring the tray?"

Kate nodded and Priya went out, the light door shutting quietly behind her. Kate piled plates and cutlery on a tray and found salad servers. She was just opening the fridge, when she heard voices coming from the hall. One sounded angry.

"I hope there's no problem with the order," Eddie was saying in the living room, "surely they can cope with a few different toppings. I'll see what's going on."

As Kate took out the salad, the hall door banged open, and a harsh voice shouted,

"Hands up!"

To her horror, Kate heard Priya's terrified cries.

"Please don't hurt me, please…"

Kate caught the heavy glass bowl as it almost slipped out of her grasp.

What was going on? She had an overwhelming desire to see. To open the door. But she stopped herself. She was even more terrified of being seen. They were in a luxury flat in a very expensive block – thoughts of hold ups and kidnapping raced through her mind. This couldn't be happening.

The loud voice continued; the speaker must've gone into the main part of the living room.

"Nobody move! I've got the gun right against her head. If you try anything…"

Priya's desperate sobbing was audible in the background.

"Who are you? What do you want?" Eddie said, his voice thick with fear.

"My name won't mean anything; I'll tell you what I want."

Something struck Kate about the man's voice. She'd heard it before, she knew it.

Priya's crying grew louder.

"Please can I sit down, I'm going to collapse, I can't..."

"Let her sit she won't do anything, please," Eddie said in an anguished tone.

"Alright, pull out that chair, but no tricks!"

The voice sounded like Adam's, but different. Harsh, angry... It couldn't be him. She must see. Once again she forced herself to stand still. Whoever it was, he didn't know she was there. She was safe in that secret room. She must stay there. She could hear everything that was going on.

"My name's Adam Trayne. You don't know me. But you should know my brother, Paul Wickfield. Or have you forgotten him?"

No one spoke.

"I'll jog your memory, De Vere, he's the boy you killed. Twenty-six years is a long time, but surely you remember that?"

"I don't know what you mean. I've never—"

"Shut up, De Vere, I'm not interested in your lies. Haven't you got the guts to own up to what you did?"

"But I didn't—"

"Be quiet – or I'll shoot her."

Kate was shaking, her mouth was dry and her heart pounded so loudly she thought everyone next door could hear it. She must do something. Adam would be facing the others in the room; he'd have his back to her. If she opened the door very quietly and came out keeping low, she'd be hidden by the island unit. She could creep round behind it to the hall and go out to get help. But the hall door was noisy, and so was the front door. If she tried to go out, he'd hear.

Adam was speaking, his words fast and forceful.

"Paul was my big brother. The brains of the family. Mum and Dad were so proud when he got into Sapplewood. They kept on about his bright future." He snorted.

"He was alright at first – for a couple of years. Then he got acne – bad."

"The others picked on him, called him names. Poxy." He spat the word. "Even his friends. He didn't want to worry Mum and Dad – Dad was ill. But he rang me all the time. He used to cry on the phone."

"Then he got an invite from this secret gang at the school. He said it was a big deal. If he passed a test he'd be in. Nobody'd bother him then."

Adam paused and Kate could hear Priya's sniffs and sobs.

"He knew you were the leader, De Vere, and the others were your mates. Isn't that true?"

"Yes, it is but..."

"So, you admit it." There was a note of triumph in Adam's voice. "He was supposed to wait outside at midnight. He said it'd be the end of all his problems.

"But it wasn't. By the next day he was dead."

Someone in the room gasped.

"You and your mates took him up to the bell tower. You must've made him drink. Got him so high he didn't know what he was doing. You made him jump or pushed him off. It's all the same."

"No, it wasn't like that..." Eddie's tone was anguished. "I never..."

"Are you telling me your gang of Silvans didn't take Paul up to the tower that night?"

"Yes, but it didn't happen the way you said..."

"Don't make excuses. When you killed Paul, you destroyed our family. My dad had another stroke and he died. I went off the rails. When my mum re-married, I changed my name. I wanted to put Paul's death behind me. But I never forgot. Or forgave you for what you did. You ruined my life, De Vere. I had to ruin yours."

Kate stood rigid with horror. Was Adam's story true? Had Eddie killed his brother?

Kate was transfixed, hardly daring to breathe. While no sounds came from next door, she exhaled and thought about the situation. Everyone in the flat was in danger. What could she do? Call the police? Her phone was in her bag on the sofa. A quick glance showed there was no landline in the kitchen, but also drew her attention to the set of knives attached to a magnetic strip on the wall. She reached over and took hold of one. At least this was a weapon, though not much good against a gun, if Adam really had one.

As if in answer, a loud scream came from the next room.

"I told you not to try anything! This gun's right against her head, if I fire... Don't think you others will get away. I'll shoot the lot of you!"

"Jeremy, don't, for God's sake!" It was Eddie's agonised voice.

"This is ridiculous. You can't – do you know who I am?" There was no mistaking Jeremy's imperious tone.

"Whoever you are – sit still. Or do you want me to shoot you first?"

Be careful, you're not in charge now, Kate thought. *If he starts shouting. Luke!* She gritted her teeth to stop them chattering. She must keep her wits about her. Was there anything she could do?

Adam spoke again.

"I suppose you're that bigshot MP – De Vere's best friend. I don't care. I'm here to destroy your life, De Vere.

"After Paul died we went to the school. Mum and Dad and me. The police asked us questions. I tried to tell them what Paul said. About the Silvans and you. But I couldn't explain properly. They didn't believe me. They said Paul made it up because he was depressed. The school wanted to keep it quiet. Of course, the police listened to them. Not a kid like me. They protected you. And your mates.

"I couldn't do anything. I was just a kid. All I wanted was to get back at you. I waited a long time. Years. My dad left me money, but I didn't touch a penny. I thought I might need it. To get even.

"You made a load of money. The beautiful wife. A son. You had it all. I waited. When I got back at you, it had to be right. In the end, I heard your son was at Sapplewood. I saw how to do it. I could get at you through him. Max."

Eddie groaned.

"Don't like to hear his name? Better get used to it. I sent money to the school. Said I was an old boy. Said the money was for a pottery studio and potter in residence. Radcliffe took the money and built the studio. I got the job.

"I watched Max. Made friends with his music teacher, Bryan. He was close to Max – very close. There was a girl from the village. Max met her at night in the woods. Busy lad. I sent him a note – like it was from Bryan. To meet him in the chapel that night.

"He was surprised to see me. I said I wanted to talk about Bryan. We went up to the tower. I had a bottle of whisky. He didn't need persuading to have a drink. In the end it was easy. I looked out – said someone was down below. Pretended to be surprised. When he leaned out..."

Then two things happened at once. Eddie let out a heart-rending wail, as if he himself had been pushed out of the tower. And the doorbell rang.

What would Adam do now? There were no sounds from the living room. Kate waited.

"Who's that?" Adam said.

"It's the pizza," Priya said.

After a pause, Adam spoke.

"De Vere – you answer the door – get rid of them. Do whatever you have to. I've got the gun against her head. Leave the door open so I can hear. And don't try anything."

Kate heard the hall door open and then the front door. She listened as the delivery guy thanked Eddie and the door closed.

"Keep your distance, De Vere," Adam said, "put them down on the table. Slowly. I'm watching you.

"Do you want to hear how your son died? I pushed him out of the tower. Just like you did to Paul. Afterwards, I was free."

Kate couldn't imagine Eddie's agony.

"When you came to the school – I saw how you looked. Sick, just like my dad. I was glad."

"You must be insane!" This was Jeremy.

"I won't tell you again – keep quiet!" shouted Adam, "I'm doing the talking. I showed you what it felt like, De Vere. How I felt. Your wife left you. You had nothing.

"I wasn't in a hurry. I stayed at Sapplewood. Might've looked dodgy to leave straightaway. After that things started to go my way. They offered me a TV show. I was riding high." Adam's voice sounded dreamy. "Riding high," he repeated.

There was a long period of silence. At least it felt long to Kate, hiding in the secret room, unable to see what was going on. She'd been standing so rigidly; her whole body was stiff. Again, she thought of creeping out. She tiptoed as far as the door, but stopped. This was madness. What could she do? If Adam saw her he might panic. Start shooting... Her thoughts chased each other round in circles. She moved away from the door, but as she did so, her elbow knocked over the plastic bottle of ketchup. The sound exploded in that small room. Adam must've heard. She clutched the worktop and held her breath. No sound came from next door.

◆ ◆ ◆

Adam spoke again. His voice had lost its dreamy quality, now it was urgent, the phrases emerging like bullets.

"I saw you at that party – the Groucho Club. You looked better than ever. And you had her. She's young – you could have another son. I didn't destroy your life. You're back at the top again.

"I smashed up the studio. But that was no good. I'll never have a chance unless you're gone.

"The gun. I meant to hand it in. But it was still there. In the drawer."

His voice rose into a screech.

"There's only one way to stop you, De Vere! You killed Paul! Now..."

Priya screamed.

◆ ◆ ◆

"Stop – he didn't do it! I saw – he didn't do it." This was Luke's voice.

Kate's heart almost stopped beating. She held onto the countertop, shaking.

Be careful!

Adam was also shocked into silence. Something in Luke's voice must've got to him. He didn't shout or threaten.

"Who are you? How do you know?"

"I was there that night. I saw it all."

Kate could feel the blood pounding in her ears. What was Luke doing? Trying to distract Adam? Or...?

"Listen to me, I can tell you exactly how it happened."

Taking Adam's silence for assent, he went on.

"Paul wasn't the only one to get an invitation from the Silvans. I was waiting outside in the dark that night as well. Two unhappy, friendless boys.

"Then they came. Four figures in long dark robes, hoods over their faces. I thought there'd be more of them, a big gang. I knew the tall one was De Vere. Everyone knew he was the leader. One of the others – he was short – had a torch and he lit our path. They didn't speak, but pointed towards the woods. We followed them.

"We came to a shed. There was wood piled up and one of them set it alight. Made a bonfire. They brought bottles out of the shed and passed them round. Wine and whisky. I drank some wine – I was used to it from home. Paul drank both. They clapped him on the back and he kept drinking.

"Then they started dancing around the fire. I felt stupid, but I joined in. I had no choice. Paul was wild. Jumping and waving his arms. He was off his head. They were clapping him.

"It went on for a long time, till one of them threw a bucket of water over the fire. They pointed for us to follow them out of the wood.

"I thought that was the end of it, but we went past the dormitory building. Past the main building. Down the path to the chapel. One of them unlocked the door and we went in. The torch showed us the way. We went up a staircase. Paul was in front of me. He kept tripping and stumbling.

"At the top there was the tower. Openings all round the sides. The night was pitch black. There wasn't much space up there for all of us. The leader pointed at me – I didn't understand what he meant. The short guy directed the torch so I could see a ledge around the outside of the tower. They wanted me to climb out onto it. Walk around the tower on it."

Kate remembered the ledge. But she'd seen it in daylight. The picture would be different in the dark.

Luke went on.

"That wasn't hard. The torch was bright. I've got a good head for heights."

She remembered him waving from high up in the tree in the bluebell wood, in another life.

"The ledge was narrow, but I held on to the tower wall for balance. The guy kept the torch beam moving ahead so I could see my way. It was easy.

"I felt strong, brave. Like I could do anything. The wine must've gone to my head. When I was nearly all the way round, I stopped. I stood up straight. Waved my hands. Called out 'Look no hands!' I was proud of myself. I'd be one of them. A Silvan."

Kate heard the exhilaration in his voice. But when he continued, the tone changed. Now sober, serious. The man was describing what the boy had seen that night.

"The Silvans weren't happy. I could tell. I saw the whole thing was a sham. They'd never let us into their gang. They just fixed on a couple of desperate boys who'd do anything to fit in. They were doing this for fun. Tormenting us. They wanted us to be terrified. But I wasn't. I'd cheated them."

"Go on," Adam said.

"It was the other boy – Paul's turn. He didn't want to climb onto the ledge. I think the alcohol had got to him. He managed to get over, but then he couldn't move. He was scared. He crouched there with his hands on the wall. The guy with the torch pointed it at him. For the first time, one of them said something. Told him to get a move on. Said he'd be a Silvan if he did it.

"He took one hand off the wall and started moving. Not proper steps. Shuffling along. A few times I thought he was going to fall. In daylight, if he hadn't been drinking, it wouldn't be hard. But up there in the dark...

"He was begging them. Saying he couldn't go on. But somehow he got the hang of it. Got into a rhythm.

"Then I said something. The wrong thing. I said..."

Luke stopped. Kate held her breath.

"I said it was easy."

"The guy with the torch heard me. The short guy. He was still moving the beam, keeping it on the ledge in front of Paul. I couldn't see his face, but I heard him say. 'This is no fun.' As if he was annoyed, disappointed."

Now Luke's words forced their way out in jerks.

"I was watching him. He was holding the torch and directing the light in front of Paul's feet. So he could see his way. Then suddenly he moved the beam. Deliberately. He shone it right into Paul's eyes.

"It blinded him. He cried out and let go of the wall. His eyes were screwed up. He stepped backwards off the ledge. His hands – his fingers were waving in the air. Grabbing... As if he was flying in the dark. But then he screamed. And fell.

"And the sound. When he hit the ground. It was terrible."

Slowly Kate exhaled. Picturing the scene. The fall.

"What did De Vere do?" Adam said.

"Nothing. None of us did anything. We just stood there. Frozen. The one who had the torch, said, 'Back to bed. Don't say anything. We weren't here. We don't know anything'. That's what we did.

"You see, De Vere didn't do it. And if I hadn't been showing off, it wouldn't have happened. The other guy wouldn't have got angry and moved the torch. It's my fault."

Again silence. Then Adam shouted.

"You're a liar! It was De Vere! He's got at you, paid you. This is all lies... I'm going to kill you... shoot you..."

Without thinking or knowing what she was doing, Kate was out of the hidden room, knife in hand, moving soundlessly across the carpet. She had the knife at Adam's neck before he realised what was happening. He was still pointing the gun at Priya, sitting on a chair in front of him.

"Adam, if you shoot I'll stick this knife in."

"What? Who's that?" He tried to turn his head.

"It's Kate. This is a knife."

"Kate? Where did you come from? What're you doing?"

"Adam, let's all calm down. Let's not have any shooting. This needs to stop. Just put down the gun, nobody needs to get hurt."

Adam seemed dazed, but he could still press the trigger at any moment.

"Please Adam, you know I'm your friend. I don't want to hurt you. Stop before this gets any worse."

He slowly moved the gun away from Priya's head. He looked at it as if uncertain what to do. Kate spoke as calmly as she could.

"Drop the gun, please Adam. We can sort this out. Find out the truth. That's what you want, isn't it? The truth?"

This seemed to get through to him. His hand fell to his side, releasing the gun onto the floor beside him. Kate kicked it away and all eyes watched it slide over the floor and disappear under a small table. There was a collective sigh of relief.

Kate kept the knife ready; Adam was unpredictable.

"I'll call the police," Jeremy was the first to recover.

"Not yet, Jeremy, this isn't finished." Kate said.

"Luke, you said it was your fault. But you didn't kill anyone. You didn't point the torch into Paul's eyes. Don't you see?"

"Yes, but if I hadn't been showing off..."

"Tell me about the other boy. The short one. Do you know who he was?"

Adam looked up sharply.

Luke shook his head.

"I never saw his face. But... I remember..." His eyes focused into the distance, as if seeing the scene. "There was one thing. When he moved the torch, the light shone for a second across his face. The hood was covering it. But I saw... the light flashed on his hair. It was blond."

Everyone was silent. Kate was the first to make the connection. She stifled a gasp, but said nothing. Her gaze shifted. Comprehension dawning, Adam slowly turned his head in the same direction. Towards the man who'd always been Eddie's best friend. Who was short. Whose hair was blond.

"You!" Adam's words burst out.

All eyes were on Jeremy Warren, his face red.

"This is all nonsense, I never... I wasn't there. Tell them, Eddie..."

Eddie looked him in the eye. He spoke quietly.

"But you were there. We never wanted to kill anyone. No one was supposed to get hurt. We'd done that sort of thing before. Okay, we were wrong to do it – of course I see that now. But Paul – that should never have happened. I don't know why you did it, I'll never understand. And I'm not going to cover up for you anymore."

"So, it really wasn't De Vere?" Adam looked dazed. "It was him?" he pointed at Jeremy.

The MP recovered quickly.

"This all happened twenty-six years ago, in the dark. With hoods. Who knows who did what? Who can say after all this time? Your brother probably fell. Moving a torch isn't murder. None of this can be proved."

Adam didn't seem to hear. He spoke to Eddie.

"I killed your son. In revenge for Paul's death. I killed the wrong man's son."

"That's not strictly true," Jeremy said, "he didn't kill your son, did he, Eddie?"

CHAPTER 12

"Jeremy, no!" Eddie's voice was a wail, "Don't!"

"We all want the truth, don't we? That's what this is all about."

What could Jeremy mean? Kate looked from one to the other. Eddie's hands covered his bowed head.

"Let me go to him," Priya sobbed.

"Of course," Kate said, keeping the knife against Adam's neck. Priya ran to Eddie and put her arms round him, kneeling on the floor by his side.

"Let me explain," Jeremy said, "we were friends at school. Eddie was... everybody liked him. A good sportsman. An 'all-rounder' they called him.

"I was flattered he wanted me to be his friend, chose me. At first. Later I got fed up – always Eddie's friend – the 'short one'. My name wasn't important. I wasn't important.

"It was the same at university. Any girl I liked, he'd come along and that would be that. He had to have it all. Never thought about what I felt. What he was doing to me. I met Ratna first, we were going out, but he pushed his way in as usual. That was too much. Why should he get away with it?

"When he was away for a few days – I met up with Ratna. Just a couple of hints that Eddie was seeing someone else... and I was there to console her. Afterwards they got back together. She found out she was pregnant. She said it was mine, but I wasn't getting involved. In the end she told Eddie it was his. He was thrilled and they got married straightaway.

"She didn't tell Eddie that Max wasn't his. He was so besotted with the boy. And I didn't care. Later on, they wanted another child and nothing happened. They had tests." Jeremy smirked, "The tests showed Eddie was completely infertile. Lowest sperm count ever." He gave a mirthless laugh.

Eddie sat with his face in his hands, Priya's arms round him.

"At first he thought Max was a miracle baby, but afterwards... In the end Ratna told him. I was the father of his beloved Max. And there'd be no more children. That finished their marriage. They just stayed together because of Max."

Eddie sat up; he spoke with a great effort.

"When I found out, I accepted Max. I loved him just as much. I was his real dad."

"How touching," Jeremy snickered.

"You're evil," Eddie broke in. He looked at Kate. "He threatened to tell Max he wasn't my son. I couldn't bear the thought. I'd do anything to stop Max finding out. Jeremy realised he had real power over me. I've hated the sight of him since then, but I had to pretend..."

He turned back to Jeremy.

"Why? You had your wife, your kids?"

Jeremy's lip curled.

"What a disappointment she turned out to be. And that pair of white rabbits. Max was different. He was good looking, popular, talented. And he was my son. I wanted to get to know him. Build a relationship."

"That's why you turned up at the school to take him out without permission."

"Why should I need your permission to take out my own son?"

"Anyway," Eddie said, "Max is dead, none of this matters."

"Yes Max is dead." Jeremy pointed at Adam, "You killed him, as you've just told us in great detail. Admitted it in front of all of us. We're witnesses. You say you've got your revenge. Was it worth it? You'll have plenty of time to ponder that question. And now I'm going to call the police."

"Just a minute, Jeremy, all in good time." Eddie stood up, and they saw he was holding the gun. "I haven't finished."

"Eddie don't... please," Priya reached out to him, but he ignored her.

"No one's doing anything till this is settled."

Eddie waved the gun in the air. He lowered it and with all eyes on him, slowly and deliberately moved the gun from one person to another. A lifetime went by as he chose his target.

Not Luke, not Luke, Kate prayed. But the hand with the gun passed Luke. And Adam. Eddie pointed the weapon directly at Jeremy. The MP's face was grey, his lips colourless.

"Eddie, you can't mean... I didn't do anything to Max. He killed Max, he's the one you want."

Eddie spoke in a cold, tight voice.

"He may've carried out the act, but it was your fault. You murdered his brother all those years ago. I never realised till now, till I heard Luke tell the story. You're a sadist, a psychopath. You enjoy inflicting pain on people. You can't be allowed to do it anymore. I'm going to stop you, now." His finger went to the trigger.

"Eddie!" It was Kate, "If you do this – what about Priya? If you go to jail... You have a chance, a life with her. Don't let Jeremy take that away from you. Then he's won."

"I won't let him get away with it," Eddie said, his voice rising.

"He won't," Kate said, "Luke will you tell the police everything you told us tonight? The whole story?"

"Yes." The reply was vehement.

"Eddie, the other boys, the Silvans, do you know their names?"

"Yes, but..."

"Don't you see? If you tell the police what happened, and so do Luke and the others – even if it was years ago, the police can still charge Jeremy. He'll go to prison."

Eddie looked at her, still pointing the gun at Jeremy. Kate held her breath, her heart thumping against her ribs. She'd done everything she could. Played her final card. The knife shook in her hand. If this didn't work...

Still Eddie said nothing. Priya was silently weeping. All eyes were on Eddie. Finally, he spoke.

"Priya, open the safe."

Gulping back the tears, she stood up and went to a painting by the window. She pulled the picture back, to reveal a safe. She entered a code into the keypad and the door swung open. Eddie walked over to the open safe and placed the gun inside. He closed the door and pushed back the picture. He took out his phone and punched in the numbers. Nine, nine, nine.

When the police left, after arresting Adam and Jeremy, and taking preliminary statements from the others, it was after midnight. Eddie insisted on sending Kate and Luke home in a taxi. They were both too overwhelmed and exhausted to talk, but sat close together, holding hands.

"I must have a coffee," Kate said once they were in her flat, "do you want one?"

He nodded. She put the mugs down on the coffee table and they drank in silence. Kate shook her head slowly.

"I should've known it was Adam."

"How could you?"

"Someone said a 'bat' came to get Max."

"So what?"

"Adam wore a long black coat with a hood and cape – we said he looked like Batman. I never put two and two together till now."

Luke put down his mug.

"Katie," he said, taking her hand, "you saved my life tonight. You were... I can't even describe how awesome you were. You took charge... You saved Jeremy's life as well. If it wasn't for you..." He paused.

"I've always loved you, ever since we were teenagers. But I felt I wasn't worthy of you. Because I'd done something wrong. Even before I remembered what happened, about Paul's death, I felt guilty. I didn't deserve to be with you.

"But you shouldn't..."

"It was just a feeling. I didn't know why. But now I see – you made me see – Paul's death really wasn't my fault."

"Not at all. Like Eddie said, Jeremy wanted Paul to fall, it was nothing to do with you. He could've done the same to you." She gulped and clutched his hand tighter.

Luke shook his head.

"He actually enjoys making people suffer."

"Max was the same." Kate told Luke everything she'd found out about the boy. "He was like his father."

They sat in silence, thinking about Max and Jeremy.

"Enough of that," Luke said, "let's talk about the future. We've –

I've wasted enough time. I don't want to wait any longer. I love you Katie, and I want us to live together as soon as possible."

His face was close to hers. Kate leaned towards him and kissed him. He put his arms round her. Tired as they were, all the years of longing came out in that kiss.

◆ ◆ ◆

EPILOGUE - Newspaper reports

MP Jeremy Warren arrested in connection with schoolboy's death

The police confirm that Jeremy Warren, MP, has been taken into custody on suspicion of murder. The incident took place 26 years ago at Sapplewood School, where 16-year-old Paul Wickfield lost his life.

Witnesses have recently come forward to identify the MP as the boy's killer.

Three months later

Wealthy entrepreneur, Eddie De Vere, marries

Eddie and his fiancée, Priya Basu, tied the knot in an intimate ceremony in the grounds of his country house.

Eddie founded a charitable trust named MASCOT in memory of his late son, Max, who tragically passed away two years ago. The trust supports talented young composers.

Six months later

Historic building destroyed by fire

A devastating fire engulfed Sapplewood School during the early hours of last night. Recently acquired by the Queensmead Group, the former boys' school was undergoing conversion into a luxury hotel.

The main building and chapel were completely destroyed, and other structures sustained extensive damage. Preliminary reports suggest the fire was caused by an electrical fault. No one was injured in the blaze.

"The land's cursed," said Steve Grant, landlord of the White Hart pub.

"The dead don't rest easy at Sapplewood."

BOOKS BY THIS AUTHOR

Now Is The Time

Yolanda has it all, or so it seems. An ambitious young lawyer set for a bright future, she's the envy of many.

But a few days at an obscure seaside town change everything. As she solves a baffling ten-year-old mystery, Yolanda discovers her real path in life and finds true love.

Will she have the courage to pursue her dreams and thwart a ruthless enemy - her own mother?

Printed in Great Britain
by Amazon

19663043R00119